The HOLLER

The HOLLER

ALICE MONDAY

Published by Jewel C Parker Press

Cover design by Madisyn Carlin with Mountain Peak Edits & Design
Developmental Edit by Madisyn Carlin with Mountain Peak Edits & Design
Copyedit by Abigail Timm with Servant's Song Publishing
Proofread by Natalie Aaron with Purple Moon Editing
E-book formatting by Abigail Timm with Servant's Song Publishing
Paperback formatting by Abigail Timm with Servant's Song Publishing

E-book ASIN: B0DVMK9SJN
E-book ISBN: 979-8992545807
Paperback ISBN: 979-8-9925458-3-8

All scriptures and quotations are taken from the King James Version Bible.

Lyrics from "What a Friend We Have in Jesus," published in 1865 by H.L. Hastings appear in Chapter 7.

https://authoralicemonday.com/

To my brother Jacob and my sister-in-law Jessica, who inspired the Jacob and Jessica of this book. Your love and devotion to one another is inspirational. May God continue to bless your marriage.

Content Warning

Please be advised that this novel includes portrayals of alcoholism consistent with its historical setting that includes moonshining during the Prohibition Era. There is no cheating and are no deaths throughout the story.

"For I have heard the slander of many: fear was on every side: while they took counsel together against me, they devised to take away my life. But I trusted in thee, O Lord: I said, Thou art my God. My times are in thy hand: deliver me from the hand of mine enemies, and from them that persecute me."

—Psalm 31:13-15

Part 1

The Snare is Set

"The proud have hid a snare for me, and cords; they have spread a net by the wayside; they have set gins for me. Selah."
—Psalm 140:5

Chapter 1

Blowing Rock, Watauga County, North Carolina, 1923

The rooster had been crowing for hours before the sun topped the ridges, but Diana Puckett was already awake. She sat at the foot of the bed, listening to catch her mother's uneven footsteps coming down the hall. A soft thud followed, then silence.

"Ma?" Diana called, bouncing up and running out into the hallway.

Margaret Puckett leaned against the wall, one hand pressed to the wood, her breath ragged. The left side of her face twitched as if her cheekbone had a mind of its own.

"Just a spell," her mother whispered, smiling as if that would chase away the truth. "It comes and goes."

Diana put her arm around her mother's elbow and steered her toward the kitchen. "You shouldn't be behaving as if everything is normal. Jacob and I can do the chores."

"I don't want to stay in bed all day, Diana," Margaret said, her speech a little slurred. "Your father needs me."

Diana restrained what she was thinking—that Pa hardly paid attention to anyone or anything anymore unless it was the bottle. Robert Puckett had once been a man of respect in his community, a deputy with his boots shined and a clean-shaven face. Now, half the time, he couldn't find his badge, and the other half of the time, he didn't care to try.

The fire in the woodstove burned low, leaving the kitchen cool. Jacob sat at the table with his long legs stretched out under it, balancing a pencil across his knuckles. His dark hair curled up in all directions as if he had just woken up.

"Y'all are late gettin' up," he teased.

"Been up," Diana answered, guiding their mother to her chair. "Ma nearly lost her balance again."

Jacob's smile faltered. He pushed his chair back and stood up. "Maybe you better lie down Ma."

"Don't start," Margaret scolded her son. Her fingers trembled as she smoothed them over the tabletop as if ironing out the wrinkles with her hands. "I've been lying down all night. I'll be fine."

The kitchen door creaked and Robert Puckett entered the house, his uniform wrinkled, and smelling like whiskey. He clapped Jacob on the shoulder—hard.

"Jacob," Robert declared, his voice booming even though the room was quiet. "You're comin' with me today. I told Martin you're not green like the other fellows. They'll want you to join the force soon enough."

Jacob's eyes flashed to his mother. "Pa, Ma needs help around here. Might I stay here and help her and Sissy with the chores today?"

"You'll do as I say," Robert commanded. "You'd better learn. A young man your age will need to take care of his own family soon. You need to learn the ropes."

Diana protested. "But Pa, I could really use Jacob's help today . . ."

"Stay out of this, Diana," Robert growled, thumping a hand on the table. Margaret winced as a spoon fell off the table, rattling on the floor.

The room went still except for the faintest pop from the fire. Diana's chest burned, but she pressed her lips together in silence. Fighting Pa now would only set him off more.

Jacob stepped forward, jaw set. "I'll come, Pa. Just let me finish breakfast."

Robert muttered something about Martin waiting, then left as abruptly as he'd entered, the door banging shut behind him.

Margaret hunched her shoulders. "I'm sorry kids. Your father is . . . stressed these days."

“Don’t you worry, Ma,” Diana said to her, although the words tasted sour on her tongue. “It will be all right.” But even as she said it, she could not help but feel that a storm was brewing in the Blue Ridge Mountains.

Chapter 2

The late morning sun hit the streets of Blowing Rock in a weak, pale glow. Deputy David Martin had been awake since long before sunrise, nursing the taste of moonshine and the memory of Robert Puckett's booming voice from that morning. Jacob's obedience had been admirable, but Martin's teeth ground together thinking of the father, once a man of respect, now a shadow swayed by pride and the bottle.

Robert Puckett had once been a friend, a partner, someone to lean on when the work got hard. Now, he brought nothing but embarrassment in his wake.

And then there was Margaret. Martin's chest tightened at the thought of her. He had seen the way she looked at Robert, and the way Robert could never truly return her love with any steadiness. It was not just Robert's drinking that was the issue. It was the man's pride and refusal to take responsibility. And still she clung to him.

Martin clenched his jaw. If Robert couldn't be trusted to serve the county, to serve his family, then someone had to make sure Margaret never suffered more than she already had.

He paused outside the sheriff's office and watched through the window as Sheriff C.M. Critcher sorted reports. Martin knew better than to step inside unannounced. He had a reputation to keep up, and he intended to maintain the facade of the dutiful deputy, the man who upheld the law.

Inside, he allowed himself a moment to pour a small measure from the flask hidden inside his coat. The burn of alcohol did little to warm him, but it steadied his hands. He told himself it was for focus. It always was.

He thought of a picture Robert had often showed him of Jacob sitting at the kitchen table with Diana. The boy had a good, strong heart, and was steady in ways that Robert never was. He deserved better than this life he was born into, but he was tethered to his father just as tightly as his mother was to her husband.

He shoved the flask back into his pocket and straightened. Today, he'd watch. He'd observe and make note of where Robert went, what he said, and what he did. Every misstep could be used and catalogued. Martin had patience. That was his advantage. One wrong move from Robert, and this whole town, maybe even the whole of Watauga County, would see the truth, and Margaret would be free from a life built on a man too weak to hold it.

Martin stepped outside and tipped his hat to the first people that passed by, holding his head high. The deputy sheriff's badge gleamed in the sunlight displaying his authority even as his mind spun with plans of putting Robert, the man who was once his closest friend, in his place: a plan that, in Martin's eyes, justice demanded.

Chapter 3

The morning fog clung to the mountains like a shroud, softening the sharp edges of the ridges, and rolling on. Drifting from the barn was the insistent thud of the milk pail and the deep, vibrating mooing of the cow. Diana stood at the fence, sweeping her stray hairs back out of her face as she watched Jacob spreading grain for the chickens.

"You ought to let me do that," she said.

"I've got it," Jacob said, tossing the last handful of grain.

"You've got Pa to fret about," Diana insisted. "You better go on now."

"You know I don't want to be a deputy." Jacob leaned on the fence as he said it, laughing at the chickens fighting over their food.

"I know, and you don't have to let him make you something you don't want to be, but I don't want you making him angry either. What if he takes it out on Ma?"

"He won't take it out on Ma," Jacob stated. "He loves Ma."

"I know he loves Ma," agreed Diana, "but Pa ain't acting right when he's drinking, and sometimes he don't know what he said or did when he sobers up again."

"I know," Jacob said as he looked up from the chickens to his sister. "That's why I gotta keep up the charade a little longer. I know Martin is Pa's friend and all, but he's been acting queer. I think he's conflicted because Pa's usually good at his job, but he can't do it real well when he's drunk all the time."

"You think Martin might say something to the sheriff?" Diana asked.

"Maybe." Jacob grimaced. "He would be right to do it, but of course, that would put us in a bind. We need Pa's money."

"I didn't know it was that bad," Diana admitted. "Maybe I can take up washing clothes for our neighbors or something."

"Nah, you need to stay here with Ma. She needs you, Di." Jacob gave his sister a half-hearted grin.

"And you? What happens when Pa screws up and Martin ain't around? Are you going to take the fall for him just because you're working with him?"

"It won't come to that, Sissy." Jacob shot her down.

"How do you know?" she insisted.

"I can't think of that, because bad as I hate to admit it, Pa is right. I don't know what I want to do with my life, and I'm being offered a job on the force as soon as I get through my training. When I'm on the payroll, I'll be able to bring what I make home to you and Ma. You know I'm right. With Pa squandering all the money away on liquor, we need it."

"And I am so grateful." Diana walked over to her brother and squeezed his shoulder as they both stared at the chickens. "But you're getting married soon, and you're going to need to take care of your wife and build your own family."

"Jessica will understand if I need to put the wedding off. I've told her what's going on. She's not ignorant of it."

"No," Diana admitted. "She's not, but Ma might never get better, and Pa might never stop drinking. You're gonna have to live your own life. You deserve to live your own life."

"I know, Sis, but with all that's been going on, I don't know if it is in the Lord's timing for me and Jessica to get married right now."

"Are you just saying that 'cause her daddy preached on God's timing last Sunday?" asked Diana.

"No." Jacob laughed. "I'm saying it because God's timing is not our own. It has nothing to do with Pastor Howard."

"If you say so." Diana remained unconvinced.

"I say so. Besides, I have faith that Pa will get better. He's only lost right now because he don't know how to best help Ma, and I'm worried about Martin. Pa might consider him a friend, but Martin's jealous. He always has been. Pa is the better deputy by far, and Martin can't stand it. With Pa showing up for work drunk—when he does show up for work, that is—it makes Martin look like a better worker than before."

"Yeah, Pa just ain't the same anymore. I see it." Diana scuffed her feet on the ground, anxious for her family's future.

Chapter 4

David Martin rode along the dirt road in his patrol wagon, eyes scanning the familiar stretches of the small town. He had been awake for hours, but sleep had not come easy. Thoughts of Robert Puckett and his family gnawed at him like a slow ache.

The Puckett homestead was half-hidden by the morning mist as he watched from a distance. The barn door swung open, and he could just make out the tall, wiry figure of Jacob moving about. Beside him, Diana tended to their mother, Margaret's small frame hunched against the chill as she was led to the fence to view the horses. Jacob and Diana were the picture of dutiful care and respect—both things their father Robert could not manage.

Martin's jaw clenched. He could hear the whispers already, even if no one had spoken them aloud just yet, about Robert neglecting his duty as a husband and father to take care of his family. Where was Robert this morning, anyway? The way Margaret looked at him, the way she leaned on him when he was sober enough to appear in public, disturbed Martin. She deserved better than what Robert could give her; she deserved stability.

Martin was a man of law and of order. That was what he told himself every day. Order required judgment, and judgment required action. Robert's failures, his drunken neglect, and his carelessness were plain for everyone to see.

Martin rode on slowly, the horse's hooves clopping steadily against the cold ground. The air was sharp, smelling faintly of smoke and pine. A dog barked somewhere in the distance. Martin drew his coat tighter, thinking back to better days when he and Robert had been true partners and shared the same patrol wagon, when they would sit out by the edge of the river talking and sharing a can of beans. Back before the moonshine. Before Margaret's sickness. Before jealousy had taken root and grown like ivy up the walls of his mind.

He could just imagine Margaret's smile, soft as the morning light through the church windows. She'd always had a kindness about her, a patience that even a man like Robert seemed worth forgiving. Martin had tried to let that go. He'd prayed it out, but even his patience for God to do something about Robert wasn't as good as Margaret's patience, so he had also drowned his sorrows in liquor—but just the one time, and not repeatedly shirking his duties like Robert had. Even so, no prayer, no liquor, no hard day's work could wash Margaret Puckett from his mind. He could offer her so much more.

The sheriff's office finally came into view. He pulled up the wagon beside the hitching post and stepped down. Inside, Sheriff Critcher was going through a stack of reports. Martin nodded a greeting and went to hang his hat on the wall.

"Mornin', Martin," the sheriff said without looking up from his work.

"Mornin', sir," Martin replied.

"You get a look at the situation up near Puckett's Holler? Feller said he saw Robert's horse parked near the Green Park Inn."

Martin's heart gave a thud, though he kept his face from showing it.

"Can't say I did, but I'll check on it."

"Do that," the sheriff said as he scribbled something on a sheet of paper. "Man's been slippin'. Shame, too. He used to be one of the best."

Martin nodded, fighting the small, wicked satisfaction curling in his gut. "I'll keep an eye on him, Sheriff."

He stepped back outside, letting the cold hit his face. He reached into his coat pocket, felt the cool metal flask, but left it there. He didn't need it. Not yet.

"Robert Puckett," he said under his breath tsk-tsking. He watched a crow land on a fence post, then disappear into the trees. "You're hanging yourself, and you don't even see it."

He adjusted his hat and climbed back into the wagon. The day stretched ahead, quiet and waiting. Somewhere in the silence, he could almost hear the Lord's voice whispering like a warning through the wind, though he wasn't sure if it was God or something darker speaking to him now.

As the wagon rolled on, the mist began to lift.

Justice, he told himself. That's what it was.

And when the time came, no one would question the man who brought order back to Blowing Rock.

Chapter 5

The next morning, Diana was hard at work carrying chicken feed sacks when she heard creaking wagon wheels. She looked outside to find Jessica Reece rolling up in a wagon, her hands at the reins.

"Mornin' Diana!" Jessica called out as Diana stepped outside the barn.

Diana grinned. Jessica was the kind of young woman who could carry sunshine with her voice.

"You're out early." Jacob appeared, climbing over the fence to meet his fiancée.

"Pa needed me to take a message into town," Jessica explained, her cheeks pink from the ride. "But I thought I would stop by first and say hello to my future husband!"

Jessica giggled as Jacob helped her down from the wagon seat, lifted her by the waist, and spun her around in circles.

Diana shook her head, but in reality, she envied her brother's relationship. She didn't have time to court a boy, and with two ailing parents to care for, she didn't know if she ever would. She figured she would become a spinster.

"How's your mama?" Jessica asked, now firmly set on the ground by Jacob.

Diana hesitated. "Somewhat better this mornin'. She's sittin' up."

Jessica nodded, her eyes softening with the same worry that Diana carried. "I've been prayin' for her."

"And we appreciate it." Jacob looked at his love, squeezing her hand tight.

The three of them lingered by the wagon. Jacob helped Jessica adjust the harness strap that had slipped loose from the horse. Diana couldn't help but notice the way her brother's face lit up around Jessica.

Lost in thoughts of her brother's happiness, Diana almost missed her mother calling out, "Diana! Jacob!"

Jacob rushed past his sister, bringing Diana's attention back to the real world.

Her heart lurched. Had her mother fallen? She ran up the steps to find her mother inside the kitchen, gripping the side of the dining table, her body trembling.

"I almost fell! You weren't here!" Margaret acted irritated, swiping her son away, even as Jacob tried to help her stand erect.

A single tear slid down Diana's face as she watched her brother guide her mother across the room to sit on the worn, yellowing sofa. Jessica looked at her knowingly. Though they were but future sisters-in-law, they had a deep connection, and Diana could tell from looking at her face that Jessica knew as well as she: Diana and Jacob would never escape the holler.

Chapter 6

The rain had come in the night, tapping steadily on the windowpanes of the sheriff's office. By morning, the air was thick with the smell of wet earth and hickory smoke. Deputy David Martin sat at the sheriff's desk, staring at the small puddle forming on the windowsill where the roof still leaked.

He had half a mind to fix it, but he didn't move. His mind was elsewhere.

Robert Puckett hadn't shown up for patrol that morning. The sheriff had noticed. He always did. But the man's patience was wearing thin.

"Martin," the sheriff had said before heading out to check on a complaint near the Deep Gap, "you make sure Puckett's where he's supposed to be. I won't have a deputy making a mockery of this office."

"Yes, sir," Martin had replied calmly and respectfully. The way a man ought to sound when he's got nothing to hide.

Now, as the clock ticked and the town began to stir, he waited, almost hoping Robert would come stumbling in through the front door, uniform wrinkled, hat in hand, and his eyes bloodshot.

The door swung open. Robert stepped in, exactly as Martin had pictured. If only he had been smelling of liquor too.

"Sheriff here?" he asked.

Martin shook his head. "He left already. He went to Deep Gap."

Robert nodded, his jaw working as if chewing on words he couldn't swallow. "Tell 'im I've been checking the Rough Ridge this morning. Feller said there were bootleggers out there."

Martin's eyes narrowed. "That's funny. The sheriff said he ain't heard of bootleggers all week."

Robert's gaze flicked up, sharp and wounded all at once. "You callin' me a liar?"

"Callin' it how I see it," Martin replied. "You ain't been yourself lately, Robert. A man can't hold a badge steady when he's holdin' a bottle instead."

Robert stiffened. His fists clenched, then fell to his side. "You think you know me, Martin? You don't know the half of what I've been through. You think you're better than me?"

"I think the Lord expects more from a man who took an oath."

Robert laughed. "The Lord expects mercy too. Maybe you forgot that."

He turned and walked out, slamming the door so hard it rattled.

Martin exhaled. Mercy. That word had haunted him for months. Mercy for a man who drank his life away? Mercy for a husband who left his wife trembling in the doorway while neighbors whispered?

No. Martin had had enough. Mercy was for the innocent.

He reached into the sheriff's desk drawer and took out a sheet of paper. He wrote:

Robert Puckett. Dereliction. Late to duty again. Possible intoxication.

The words steadied him. They made it real, official truth on paper.

He set the pencil down and looked out the window. The rain had stopped. Steam rose off the rooftops as the sun began to break through the clouds, casting sharp light over the wet street.

Across the road, he saw Margaret Puckett walk into Coman's Drug Store, her shawl wrapped tight around her shoulders. Even from a distance, he could see the limp in her step.

Martin's chest tightened. He thought of going to help her, of carrying her basket, of saying something kind. Anything to make her see there were still good men left in Watauga County.

But he didn't move. He stayed behind the glass, watching her disappear into the store.

It was better this way. A man had to keep his distance if he was going to make things right.

And Martin intended to make things right. One way or another.

He turned back to the desk, picked up his pencil again, and underlined Robert's name once more, this time, hard enough to tear the paper.

Chapter 7

Sunday morning started just the way Sundays always started: with boots scraping along dirt roads, wagons groaning when wheels rolled over rocks, and families drifting up to the tiny, white Mount Bethel Church. Droning and deliberate, the church bell sounded, its echoey note carrying through the holler.

Diana walked alongside her mother, steadying her arm as they climbed the stairs to the entrance. Margaret had insisted on coming, despite her difficulty with walking; particularly her right foot's tendency to catch the edge of every step. Jacob led the way ahead of them with Jessica, his shoulders squared as if he was already the head of the family. Pa trailed behind, hat sitting low to cover his bloodshot eyes, his gait uneven as he walked.

Inside, the pews filled fast with their neighbors. Diana escorted her mother to a pew in the center of the sanctuary.

Pastor Howard stood behind the altar. Though Jessica walked in with Jacob, once inside, she left him to sit on the front pew under the close watch of her father. Pastor Howard's disapproval of her engagement to Jacob was no secret, but he allowed it because his late wife and Margaret had been the best of friends. Pastor Howard thought that the Pucketts were poor, and Robert Puckett's drinking and erratic behavior made him a man of questionable character.

Once, Jessica had admitted to Diana that her father thought marrying into the Puckett family would only cause her hardship. Diana found Pastor Howard's opinion amusing, because for her brother Jacob, Jessica was the epitome of hope. Jessica looked backward and smiled at Diana across the aisle. Diana smiled back, thankful that she had not given up on their friendship or her relationship with Jacob.

Diana was so lost in her thoughts, that she barely registered when the service began and Pastor Howard asked everyone to sing. The congregation rose, except for Margaret and a few other ailing congregants who could not stand for long. Voices swelled, filling the rafters with the first lines of "What a Friend We Have in Jesus."

What a friend we have in Jesus
All our sins and grief to bear
What a privilege to carry
Everything to God in prayer . . .

When the deacon reached their pew with the offering plate, Robert waved the man away. Diana watched Pastor Howard witness the encounter from his place at the front of the room. He shook his head, and Diana rolled her eyes. The Pucketts weren't the only ones hurting for money, but she never saw Pastor Howard shaking his head at the others.

When the last notes faded, Pastor Howard opened his Bible at the pulpit. "Brethren, this world is full of snares for the soul," he began, "and none so dangerous as the temptation found in strong drink."

At his words, Jacob and Diana glanced sideways at one another. It was obvious to them that Pastor Howard's sermon was directed at their Pa.

"The Scripture tells us plainly: *'Wine is a mocker, strong drink is raging: and whosoever is deceived thereby is not wise,'*" he quoted from Proverbs. His gaze swept over the room, but he paused a moment to stare directly at Robert Puckett. Diana watched congregants lower their faces in shared embarrassment.

Diana felt her face warm. Everyone in Blowing Rock knew her father's weakness for the bottle. In fact, most people in the whole of Watauga County knew.

"Drunkenness destroys men, families, and entire communities," Pastor Howard thundered. "It tears down what God has built. We must stand firm, guarding our homes, our children, and our faith from its poison."

His proclamation was met with several "Amens" from the audience.

Diana bowed her head, though her hands clenched tightly in her lap. Did Pastor Howard mean to make a fool of her father? Was it worth it to embarrass the entire family, including his wife and children, who did not partake in nor support Robert's drinking habit?

It seemed to Diana that Pastor Howard's sermon would never end. When it finally came to a close, Diana noticed Jessica's eyes glistening as her father called her forward to sing the closing hymn. Diana caught her gaze and gave her a small nod, a silent promise that no matter what came, they would stick together.

Chapter 8

Deputy Martin slipped quietly into the back pew of the church just as the congregation began to settle. His badge glinted beneath his coat, though he'd tucked it away so as not to draw attention. He was on duty, yes, but Sundays were different. Folks expected deputies to be watchful but also good Christians.

From the back row, he could see everything and everyone, especially the Pucketts.

The rain-washed morning light filtered through the tall church windows, giving the room a soft glow. The wooden pews creaked as families leaned in close, opening their hymnals with a rustle like leaves turning in a breeze.

Martin's eyes fixed on the Puckett family near the front.

Robert sat slumped beside Margaret; his hair was uncombed, and he was half-sober at best. The man leaned on his wife as though she were a post holding up the entire roof. Margaret, pale and trembling from her ailment, attempted to brace herself beneath his weight, though she clearly lacked the strength.

Her shoulders tipped under his weight, and she sank into the pew. Jacob immediately leaned across her, steadying his father with a firm, practiced grip. Diana laid a gentle hand on her mother's shoulder, whispering something meant to soothe.

Martin's jaw tightened. There it was. The whole miserable picture.

Robert Puckett was now too hungover to sit through preaching without dragging his wife down with him, while Margaret was trying to be strong for everyone when she was the one who needed help the most.

Martin felt the pull of anger in his chest

Pastor Howard stepped up to the pulpit, clearing his throat. He opened his Bible, thumbed through the familiar pages, and looked out over the congregation with stern, judgment-heavy eyes.

A few heads turned toward Robert as Howard started his sermon. Martin stifled a chuckle.

A bold move.

A pointed one.

Pastor Howard didn't call a man out by name, but everyone in the church knew exactly who the message was meant for.

Martin folded his arms, leaning back. So, Howard Reece had the nerve to preach against the Pucketts and yet allowed his own daughter to be engaged to the Puckett boy?

Inconsistency irritated him more than sin.

He made a mental note to speak to Pastor Howard later and figure out what the man really thought about the Pucketts—about Jacob, about Margaret's sickness, and about Jessica's future with that family.

The congregation rose slowly to sing, "What a friend we have in Jesus . . ."

Voices filled the sanctuary, soft, earnest; Southern Appalachian voices, rising and falling like the wind running across the mountains. As the second verse began, Martin slipped out through the church door, quiet as a fox leaving a henhouse.

Chapter 9

The congregation spilled out into the crisp, mountain air as the sound of voices filled the churchyard. Autumn had come to Watauga County too soon. Golden, red, and orange leaves shimmered in the sunlight like coins scattered over the hills.

The air had a bite to it that belonged to October, not September, and Diana pulled her sweater tighter around her arms. She lingered with Jessica near the stone wall that bordered the little church, waiting for their families to make their way down the steps. The church bells had stopped ringing, but congregants lingered as they visited with one another and discussed Pastor Howard's sermon.

Jessica looked past Diana, to where Jacob stood talking with one of the older men in town. He had his hat in his hands, turning it slowly with his fingers. Diana watched as his eyes met Jessica's. Then, her brother excused himself from his conversation and started walking toward them, his boots crunching twigs and a few newly fallen leaves beneath his feet.

"Jacob," Jessica said as he approached. His expression softened at her voice. "I'll be heading to Boone tomorrow morning for class at Appalachian Training School," she continued. "You ought to come by for a little bit this afternoon. I won't see you again until next Saturday."

Jacob nodded. "I'd like that." His voice was warm.

Pastor Howard had just finished shaking his hands with a deacon when he turned at the sound of his daughter's voice, overhearing her conversation with Jacob. His smile faded as he took in the little circle they had made.

"Jessica, you have packing to do tonight and need to get in bed early for a good night's rest. Don't be distracted," he warned as he brushed a speck of dust from his sleeve.

"I'll have time enough, Papa," Jessica assured him. "We'll just sit and visit for a while. Diana's coming, too. Aren't you, Diana?" Her friend turned to her, eyes widened meaningfully.

When Diana's best friend and her brother started courting, she could not have foreseen her role as perpetual chaperone, nor how often she would feel like a piece of furniture dragged into a room that makes everyone feel comfortable.

"I reckon I am," she said with a small sigh.

Pastor Howard nodded curtly, his eyes flicking at Jacob once again with disapproval. He said nothing else, though his jaw wiggled as if he was holding back the words that he really wanted to say.

A pair of women passed behind them, lowering their voices as they walked by, but not low enough. Diana caught wind of their words. "That no account Robert Puckett is a disgrace to his family coming to church after drinking like that. Poor Margaret . . ."

Diana felt Jacob go still beside her. He had heard the women, too.

Pastor Howard cleared his throat loudly, and the women hurried their pace.

"You be home before dark," Pastor Howard said to Diana. "Both of you," he specified, looking directly at Jacob.

"Yes sir," Diana and Jacob answered simultaneously.

"Stop by at three o'clock?" Jessica asked them.

"Three sounds just fine. We'll be there." Jacob gave his betrothed a warm smile.

Pastor Howard nodded at the plans they made. "That works well. I'll be inside. The three of you can visit on the porch and take advantage of the warmer weather while we still have it. It gets cooler every day."

"Thanks, Papa." Jessica smiled brightly up at her father. "We'll head out now. I'll go home to start us some lunch and pack a little."

"I need to speak with a few more folks before I leave here," Pastor Howard said as he looked around then directed his gaze toward Jacob. "Will you walk Jessica as far as Glen Burney Falls on your way home? I see your parents have already left."

"Of course." Jacob nodded.

Diana hugged her friend's shoulder. "Come on, Diana. Maybe we can stop for five minutes and put our toes in the water while we can still stand it." The girls giggled together.

"Bye, Papa," Jessica said to her father.

"Goodbye, Pastor Howard," Diana said as they began to walk away. She watched as Jacob threw up a hand to his future father-in-law before following after them.

Chapter 10

Deputy David Martin stepped out onto the church steps, adjusting his coat collar against the brisk mountain wind that could easily carry a fire far and wide. An idea sparked for him, and though he had intended to slip out of the church service early under the guise of deputy's duties, he decided to wait around and talk to the pastor first.

Soon enough, the congregation spread across the churchyard with families greeting one another, the children running around the gravestones, and women gathering in gossiping clusters that pretended not to gossip.

Martin didn't mingle. He remained on the steps, hands clasped behind his back with the quiet hunger of a man studying everything that might serve his purpose. He watched Jacob stand talking with old Mr. Quillen. Diana lingered by the stone wall with Jessica Reece. Margaret, frail and leaning heavily on her cane, was led slowly down the steps by another sister in Christ. Robert trailed behind, eyes glazed, pretending to be steady though the sway of his shoulders betrayed him.

Martin bit the inside of his cheek. Shameful! The man had no business calling himself a father, much less a deputy.

His attention snapped back to Jacob as the boy crossed the yard toward Jessica.

Jessica smiled up at him. Jacob's shoulders relaxed at her soft and warm demeanor. For just a moment, he didn't look like a young man burdened by his father's failures. He looked hopeful when he was with her.

Martin eavesdropped as Jessica invited Jacob to visit her that afternoon, heard the way the boy's voice softened toward her, and then Pastor Howard turned.

The pastor's face stiffened as he approached them, his eyes narrowing at Jacob.

Martin watched the exchange with keen interest, leaning slightly on the railing.

Jessica insisted that Diana would be there, too. "Just visiting," she said with a lightness that didn't fool her father for a second.

Howard's jaw worked as though grinding bone. He nodded eventually, but the disapproval of the Puckett boy radiated from him like heat.

Martin's eyes narrowed. There it was again. That strange tension between Howard and Jacob.

If Pastor Howard truly disapproved of the Pucketts, and it was clear that he did, why did he allow the engagement at all? Why let his daughter be pulled into the crumbling mess Robert Puckett had made of his family?

Martin watched Jessica and Diana walk away, Jacob following a few paces behind as the young women giggled together. Howard lingered, eyes fixed on Jacob as he walked away.

Martin tipped his hat toward the pastor as he descended the steps. "Fine service today, Pastor," he said.

Howard nodded stiffly. "The Lord pressed something on my heart."

"I could tell," Martin replied, careful to keep the polite respect in his tone, lest the pastor decide to bring up his leaving the service early. "If you've got a minute later, sir, I'd like to speak with you privately."

Howard's eyes flashed just slightly, a warning or a question, but he nodded. "We'll talk. Come by my house later."

"Yes, sir. Thank you, sir," Martin nodded his head goodbye. Very soon, he thought, the truth would reveal itself one way or another.

Chapter 11

The afternoon sun slanted low across Pastor Howard Reece's front porch, warming the wide plants beneath their feet. Diana sat on the top step with her hands folded in her lap, watching the dust rise on the road beyond the yard. The air smelled of cut grass and old wood, safe and familiar, the kind of place that made a person want to stay awhile.

Jessica sat beside her, shoes kicked off, toes brushing the porch railing. Jacob leaned against one of the posts, hat resting on his knee.

"I miss you both something fierce when I'm away at school," Jessica explained. "Boone feels awfully lonely without you."

Diana smiled faintly. "Sometimes I wish I was there with you. If things were different—if Ma didn't need me so much—I reckon I'd like to go to the Training School too."

Jessica turned to her, eyes bright. “You would be so good at it, Diana. You’re patient and kind. Children would take to you right off.”

Diana shrugged, though the thought settled warmly in her chest.

“Maybe one day.”

Jessica reached for Jacob’s hand. “When Jacob and I are married, I’ll help care for your mother. Like Ruth did for Naomi. I won’t leave her to struggle.”

Diana swallowed hard at that. “You’d do that?”

“I already consider her my family,” Jessica said simply. “And when the time comes, it’ll be your turn to go to school.”

Jacob shook his head slowly. “It ain’t right,” he said. “It ain’t right for either of you to carry this. Not Ma’s sickness. Not Pa’s drinking. None of it.”

Silence stretched between them.

Diana looked down at her hands. “Pa didn’t used to be like this,” she said quietly.

Jacob shook his head. “No. He didn’t.”

He stared out toward the yard, jaw tight. “Pa never touched the drink before Ma got sick. Not even a drop. He worked hard. Took pride in his badge and took pride in us.”

Jessica leaned forward slightly to listen.

“When the doctor told him there wasn’t no cure,” Jacob continued. “It was like somethin’ in him just . . . stopped. He still goes to work, well, sometimes anyway, but only out of habit. It's like he doesn't have anything left to work for."

Diana felt the familiar ache bloom in her chest.

"Sometimes," Jacob went on, "it's like he's forgotten he has children to care for. He's forgotten he has a family at all. In some ways, he acts like Ma already died, even though she is still right there in front of him."

Jessica's eyes filled with tears. She pressed her hand to her mouth.

"That's why I stay," Jacob said. "That's why I go along with Pa and Martin and all of it. Somebody's got to remember Ma's still alive. Somebody's got to hold things together."

Diana looked up at him then, her brother who carried too much for one young man. "You shouldn't have to do that alone."

"I know," he said softly.

For a moment, none of them spoke. The sun dipped lower. Somewhere inside the house, a floorboard creaked.

Diana didn't know why, but she felt suddenly afraid of how fragile everything was, of how easily a family could unravel when one thread gave way.

She tucked that fear deep inside her and lifted her chin.

"We'll get through it," she said. "All of us."

Jacob smiled, but it didn't quite reach his eyes.

Chapter 12

Deputy David Martin waited until the afternoon shadows stretched long across the churchyard before he approached the parsonage. The Reece house sat just beyond the trees, white clapboard weathered by years of wind and prayer. The porch was empty now. Whatever gentle visiting had taken place there earlier had passed on like a breeze.

Pastor Howard Reece answered the door himself.

"Yes?" he said, his voice guarded.

"Afternoon, Pastor," Martin replied, tipping his hat. "You said we might talk."

Howard studied him a moment, then stepped aside. "Come in."

The house smelled of old books and lemon oil. A Bible lay open on the small table near the window, its pages weighted with a pressed leaf. Martin took note of everything.

Howard gestured to a chair. "What is it you wanted?"

Martin did not sit right away. "I wanted to speak with you about the Pucketts."

The pastor's jaw tightened. "I reckoned as much."

Martin eased into the chair at last, folding his hands loosely in his lap. "You preached hard this morning."

"I preached the truth," Howard said sharply. "If the shoe fits . . ."

"It did," Martin said. "Plain as day."

Howard sighed and turned away, resting his hands on the back of another chair. "Robert Puckett is a stumbling block to his family and to the town. And especially to my daughter."

"Then you don't approve of the engagement."

"I never did," Howard said. "I warned Jessica. A man may be good-hearted, but blood runs deep. I've seen what drinking does to a family."

"Jacob's not his father," Martin said mildly.

"No," Howard admitted. "But he's carrying his father's burden. And that kind of weight can bend even the strongest man."

"Martin nodded as if in agreement. "You noticed then, how much responsibility the boy's taken on."

"I have," Howard said. "Too much for his age. I worry for him, but my greater concern is my daughter. I will not see her bound to a family already falling apart."

Martin rose slowly from his chair. “Then we are in agreement.”

Howard frowned. “About what?”

“That something must be done.” Martin said. “For Jessica’s sake. For the good of the town.”

Howard searched his face. “You are a man of the law.”

“I am,” Martin replied. “And the law exists to keep order. Sometimes that means stepping in where others have failed.

Howard’s lips pressed into a thin line. “I won’t bear false witness.”

“I wouldn’t ask you to,” Martin said smoothly. “Only to speak the truth, should the time come.”

Finally, Howard nodded once. “If Jacob Puckett brings harm upon himself or my daughter, I will not shield him.”

“That’s all I needed to hear,” Martin said, tipping his hat.

As he stepped back outside, the sky had darkened to the color of bruised fruit. The air felt charged, like a storm waiting to break.

Martin walked down the path with steady steps.

Two men of influence now shared the same understanding, even if one of them did not yet realize how far that understanding would be stretched.

And somewhere beyond the trees, the Puckett family carried on, unaware that lines had been quietly drawn.

Chapter 13

The road home felt longer than it had that morning.

Diana walked beside Jacob as the sun dipped low behind the ridgeline, the sky streaked with pink and purple. Leaves crunched beneath their boots, and the wind carried that sharp scent of autumn smoke from somewhere down the valley. She tried to talk herself out of the feeling pressing against her ribs, but it wouldn't ease.

Something had shifted.

"You're quiet," Jacob said at last.

Diana shrugged. "I'm just tired."

He glanced at her sideways but didn't press. Jacob never did when he sensed she was holding something back. That had always been their way. Quiet understanding instead of questions.

Behind them, Pastor Howard's house disappeared around a bend. Diana thought of the way his eyes had followed them as they left the porch. He was not angry or unkind, but it unsettled her more than anger ever could.

"You going with Pa tomorrow?" she asked.

Jacob nodded. "Martin said he wanted me to ride along again. Just routine."

Diana stopped walking.

Jacob turned. "What?"

"I don't like that," she said, the words tumbling out before she could stop them. "You keep sayin' it's routine, but it don't feel like it. Not anymore."

Jacob smiled gently. "Di, Martin's just doin' his job."

"That's what scares me," she said. "He watches too close. He remembers too much, and he don't look at folks the way other people do."

Jacob studied her face, searching for the right response. "You're seein' shadows because things are hard right now."

"Maybe," she admitted. "But sometimes shadows mean there's somethin' solid standing in the way of the light."

Jacob laughed softly. "You've been listenin' to too many of Pastor Howard's sermons."

"Maybe you ain't listenin' to them well enough," she shot back, then immediately softened. "I'm sorry. Just promise me you'll be careful."

"I promise," he said.

But those two words felt thin in the cooling air.

When they reached home, Margaret sat by the window, watching the last of the daylight fade. Her face was pale.

"You're back," she said.

Jacob bent to kiss her cheek. "Wouldn't miss supper."

Diana went to the stove, stirring the pot, though it was already done. She watched her mother from the corner of her eye. Margaret's left hand trembled harder than usual, her fingers curling inward as if they didn't quite belong to her anymore.

After supper, Jacob stepped outside to fetch water. Diana dried the last plate, her mind still churning.

"Ma," she said quietly. "Did Pastor Howard say anything to you today?"

Margaret should her head. "No. Why?"

"I just wondered."

Margaret studied her daughter's face. "You feelin' uneasy again?"

Diana nodded.

Margaret reached out, resting her trembling hand over Diana's. "The Lord don't give us warnings for nothin' child. But He also don't ask us to live in fear."

"I'm tryin'," Diana whispered.

Later, as night settled over the holler, Diana stood at the doorway watching Jacob cross the yard for one last check on the animals in the barn. The lantern light caught his face for just a moment. It was steady, kind, and unaware.

She pressed her hand to the doorframe and whispered a prayer. One that was not polished or pretty, but desperate.

“Lord, keep him safe.”

Chapter 14

Deputy David Martin did not hurry.

That was the first thing he had learned about difficult work, that you moved steady but never fast.

Rushed men made mistakes. Patient men shaped outcomes.

The lantern on the desk cast a dull circle of light across the sheriff's office as he reviewed the ledger one last time. Dates, times, and names were written on it neatly. Everything was orderly. Truth, when written carefully enough, had a way of becoming permanent.

He closed the book and stood up, slipping on his coat. Outside, the night had settled thick and cold, the kind that pressed close to a man's thoughts. The moon was only a sliver, barely enough to light the road as he mounted his horse.

Jacob Puckett would be waiting.

Martin followed the ridge path instead of the main road, guiding the horse with practiced ease. He knew these hills better than most. He had patrolled them for years before Robert had lost his footing.

The barn came into view just ahead, the lantern growing faint through the cracks in the boards. Jacob stood near the water trough, sleeves rolled up, hands busy with a task.

“Evenin’ Jacob,” Martin called out.

Jacob turned toward him. “Evenin’ Martin.”

“I’m off duty now. Thought I’d come see y’all for a spell.”

Jacob nodded. “Everything all right?”

Martin smiled. “That depends on the man answerin’ the question.”

They stood there for a moment, the horse shifting behind him, the night breathing around them.

“I spoke with Pastor Howard today,” Martin said casually.

Jacob stiffened.

“He’s worried,” Martin went on. “About Jessica. About the path she’s settin’ her feet on.”

“He’s always been worried,” Jacob replied. “I get that. No man is good enough for a father’s daughter.”

“Yes,” Martin agreed. “But this time, he spoke plain.”

Jacob set down a bucket. “What’s that supposed to mean?”

"It means," Martin said evenly, "that a young man carryin' another man's shame risks passin' it on. Folks are watchin', Jacob. Closely."

Jacob held his ground. "This is about the sermon. About my Pa. I ain't done anything wrong. I don't drink like him."

Martin nodded. "Yes, but you know as well as I do that good men often get caught in the middle, and when the law comes knockin', intentions don't count for much."

The lantern light flickered. Somewhere in the trees, an owl called.

"The sheriff has asked me to keep close watch on your Pa," Martin continued. "Because of your father's conduct. He's been missing work. His patrols are irregular."

Jacob swallowed. "Pa's sick at heart. That don't make him a criminal. It just makes him a bad employee."

"It makes him a liability."

The words landed heavy between them.

"I'm tellin' you this as a kindness," Martin added. "If things turn sour, it's best you ain't standing too close when they do."

Jacob searched his face. "Why are you suddenly so concerned about me, Robert? Are you threatenin' me?"

"No, boy, I'm warnin' you. You know I've only ever wanted what's best for your Pa. He's my partner, but right now, he's not fit to protect and serve. It ain't my job to fire him. Seems to me the sheriff keeps him on simply 'cause he feels sorry for him, but it's only a matter of time before something bad happens cause he's drinking on the job."

He turned his back toward his horse. "Ride with me tomorrow. There's a matter near Hanna's Store that needs looking into. The sheriff'll appreciate the help."

After a moment, Jacob nodded. "All right."

Martin mounted his horse. "Good. I'll see you at first light."

As he rode away, the barn lantern dimmed behind him.

Chapter 15

The morning came soft and gray, the kind of morning that muffled all sound. Fog pressed low against the holler, curling around the house and settling into the trees to stay.

Diana rose before the rooster again, pulling on a sweater and tying her hair back with a ribbon that had long since lost its color.

Her mother sat at the table when Diana entered the kitchen, hands wrapped around a mug.

"You didn't wake me," Diana said.

"I didn't want to trouble you. You need to sleep," Margaret said.

Diana set water on the stove to boil fresh and began slicing bread. "Jacob's ridin' out early with Martin."

"I know," Margaret said. "He told me."

Diana paused. "You don't like it either, do you? I get that Jacob thinks it's solid employment, but it seems to me like he's just doing Pa's job for him."

Margaret's fingers tightened around her cup as she brought it to her lips. "I don't like much of anything lately."

They shared a quiet look between a daughter and her mother, bound together by a worry that neither could name aloud.

When Jacob came in, he was already dressed for the day, boots polished and his jacket buttoned tight. He looked older somehow.

"Breakfast'll be ready in a minute," Diana said.

"That's all right," he replied. "Martin'll be waitin' outside."

He bent to kiss their mother's cheek. Margaret touched his face with her trembling hand.

"Be careful," she whispered.

"I will," he promised.

Diana walked him to the door.

"You don't have to go," she said. "You know that, don't you?"

"I do. You know I do," he pleaded with his sister.

The day stretched on. Diana washed clothes, swept the floor, and tended to her mother between her spells. Margaret's hands failed her twice before noon, and her legs eventually stiffened so that Diana had to help her to the bed.

By midafternoon, the fog had lifted just enough to reveal the ridge line. Diana stepped outside, shading her eyes.

Jacob should've been home by now.

She told herself not to fret. Men got delayed and patrols often took longer than expected. Still, she watched the road.

When evening came without him, she began to feel extra uneasy.

Supper went untouched. Margaret sat rigid at the table, staring at the door as if willing it to open.

"He'll come," she said, though her voice wavered.

Diana went out into the yard at dusk, her heart pounding. She remained in the barn with the animals until the lantern burned low, hoping to hear the hoofbeats of her brother's horse arrive.

When Diana had to light the lantern again, she knew something had to be wrong.

Chapter 16

Deputy David Martin did not rush when the alarm bell rang. The smell of smoke had reached him long before the sound.

By the time he stepped outside the sheriff's office, the glow was visible over the ridge.

Blowing Rock would remember this night.

Martin mounted his horse and rode toward town at an even pace. Fires had a way of making people reckless. He had no intention of being counted among them.

When he arrived, half of Blowing Rock's residents were already moving in action. Men shouted as they passed buckets hand to hand. Flames licked hungrily at the edge of the dry, wooden roof of the mercantile, Hanna's Store, the exchange building, and the Episcopal reading room. The fire had extended down the row of buildings along Main Street, nearly making its way to H.C. Hayes' store as well.

Martin dismounted and took in the scene with a practiced eye.

Order first. Panic later.

"Where're the Pucketts? Aren't they with you?" someone asked him.

Martin tried to look concerned. "On duty," he said. "Or they were."

His comment took root immediately.

By dawn, the fire lay smoldering, half of Hanna's storefront blackened and ruined. Men stood in the street coughing from the smoke in their lungs. The sheriff arrived late.

By midmorning, Robert Puckett was located passed out behind the row of burned buildings, smelling of liquor.

When the townspeople accused him of arson, Robert's shoulders sagged as if the words confirmed what he already believed about himself.

Martin watched it happen with something like pity, but then Jacob appeared, his face gray with ash and exhaustion. Turned out, he'd been helping the crowd try to put out the fire.

The boy stepped forward. "I done it." Jacob said, his voice steady. "Pa didn't have nothin' to do with it."

The crowd went quiet

Robert's head snapped up. "Jacob—"

"We were behind the mercantile. I was angry with my Pa for drinking," Jacob continued. "I took his bottle of liquor and threw it up against the wall of the building to break it. Then, I set the shards of glass on fire. I didn't count on the fire spreading."

Martin felt the moment lock into place, solid as iron.

Sheriff frowned. "Son, you best think carefully. I know you're smart enough to know that alcohol is flammable. You wouldn't do that."

"But I did," Jacob said. "I didn't think. I was angry with my Pa. It's my fault, and if you fine me, I won't have the money to pay you back. You'll have to take me in."

Robert's mouth opened, then closed again. His eyes filled with tears, but he said nothing.

Martin stepped forward at last, slow and deliberate. "Jacob, you understand what you're sayin?"

"Yes, sir."

"And you're willin' to sign a statement?"

Jacob nodded.

Martin handed him a piece of paper.

Jacob took the pen.

When the cell door closed behind Jacob later that afternoon, the sound echoed louder than it ought to have. Martin stood outside, hands folded behind his back, watching the boy settle onto the narrow bench.

Jacob looked up. Their eyes met.

"I warned you, boy. Now, you're paying the price for the sins of your father. What will your mother think?" Inside, Martin felt the town tilt subtly in his favor.

He had warned the boy. He'd done his part. It wasn't his fault Jacob took the blame for his father's misdoing.

Justice, he told himself, required sacrifice. The Pucketts had plenty to spare.

Chapter 17

Deputy Martin arrived at the Puckett's just before dusk.

Diana saw him from the window. The sight of him sent a cold threat straight through her chest. She wiped her hands on her apron and stepped on the porch before he could knock.

"What's happened?" she asked.

Martin removed his hat. His face was solemn in a way that looked practiced. "There's been a fire in town."

Her heart stuttered. "Pa? Jacob? We haven't seen Pa in days, and Jacob didn't come home last night."

Martin hesitated, just enough to appear concerned. "Your brother's been taken into custody."

The words struck like a physical blow. This was not what she had expected.

"For what?" Diana asked.

"Arson," he said.

"No. That can't be right. Jacob would never intentionally set something on fire."

"He confessed," Martin clarified.

Diana stared at him, searching for information not given. "Jacob wouldn't . . ." she began to protest some more, but Martin cut her off.

"I suspect he was tryin' to protect your father," Martin said.

Behind her, the door creaked open. Margaret stood there, pale and trembling, one hand braced against the frame.

"My son?" she asked.

Martin shifted his weight. "He's alive and safe, but he's being held until the sheriff sorts the matter."

Margaret's knees buckled. Diana ran to her and held her upright with all her strength.

"You knew," Diana said suddenly, turning back to Martin. "You knew he'd step in to save Pa. Why'd you let him do it?"

Martin met her gaze. "I knew Jacob Puckett could be a good man."

"A good man don't belong in a jail cell," Diana shot back.

"Sometimes," Martin replied, "good men pay for bad ones."

The words settled between them like ash.

"Can I see him?" Diana asked.

"Not today," Martin said. "Tomorrow."

He replaced his hat. "I'm sorry, Diana."

He tipped his hat outward to her mother. "Margaret."

He felt Diana's eyes on him as he walked away, the lie of that apology ringing louder than the fire bell that they didn't hear so deep in Puckett's Holler.

***

That night, Diana sat beside her mother's bed, holding her through every trembling spell. Pa still hadn't come home yet.

When her mother finally grew still with sleep, Diana did not.

She opened her Bible to the Psalms. Her finger traced words of King David, a man who had been hunted and pursued yet still clung to God.

"Hide me from the secret council of the wicked," she read.

A fire had been set, and a confession had been given. Somewhere between those two truths, there was a lie. Justice had been bent.

Diana closed the book and looked into the dark.

If the law would not save her brother, then she would.

Part 2

Smoke Over Blowing Rock

"Behold, thou desirest truth in the inward parts: and in the hidden part thou shalt make me know wisdom."
–Psalm 51:6

Chapter 18

Martin stopped in the sheriff's office. Sheriff Critcher sat hunched over his desk, rubbing his temples.

"Has the boy slept?" Martin asked.

"Like the dead," the sheriff muttered. "Didn't say a word after you left.

Martin nodded. "That's consistent."

"Still don't sit right," the sheriff said. "This young man confessin' so quick."

Martin leaned against the door frame. "Jacob Puckett is a protector. That family runs on sacrifice. Everyone knows that."

The sheriff sighed. "The town's restless."

"They'll settle," Martin said. "They always do once the story's fixed."

The sheriff looked up. "Fixed?"

"Finished," Martin corrected smoothly.

He stepped back out onto the street. The town looked different after the fire. The burned storefronts loomed, their blackened beams standing like broken ribs. The town would rebuild. What mattered was why they believed it had burned.

By midmorning, Martin paid a visit to Pastor Howard Reece.

The parsonage was neat as a ledger. Pastor Howard answered the door, his Bible already in hand as if expecting company.

"Deputy," he said stiffly.

"Pastor," Martin replied. "May I come in?"

Howard hesitated, then stepped aside.

They sat across from one another at the small dining table. Sunlight streamed through the window, illuminating dust drifting to the floor.

"I won't take much of your time," Martin said. "I wanted to speak with you about Jacob Puckett."

Howard's jaw tightened. "I've prayed on it."

"As have I," Martin lied. "The problem is, Jacob has confessed to the recent fire."

"So I've heard."

"He did so to protect his father," Martin continued. "A lying sin born of loyalty. He was misguided, but he is not malicious."

Howard looked down at his Bible. "At this point, my concern is for my daughter."

"As it should be," Martin went on. "I recommend a period of separation for her sake, and for the church's.

It won't look good if the pastor is standing by an arsonist that caused the destruction of our beloved town's business district."

Howard remained silent. At last he said, "The Lord disciplines those He loves."

"Yes," Martin said softly. "And sometimes He uses me to do it."

When Martin left the parsonage, the decision had already been made.

By afternoon, word had traveled quickly and efficiently. When Jessica returned from the teacher's college for the weekend, her visits with Jacob Puckett would cease. Appearances would be kept.

Martin returned to the jail just before supper. He stood outside Jacob's cell, hands clasped behind his back.

"You all right?" he asked.

Jacob nodded. "Yes, sir."

"You've done a hard thing," Martin said.

Jacob looked up at him from his place on the bench. "I just don't want my family to hurt no more."

Martin didn't answer right away.

"What happened to my Pa?" he continued.

"He was questioned," Martin said finally, "and then released. The sheriff thought it best if he go home."

Jacob exhaled, relief softening his shoulders. "Thank you. I hope what I've done for him will get him to see that he's got to change his ways."

Martin watched him for a moment.

"Sheriff Critcher let him go, Jacob. After the whole town saw him drunk, and not helping put out the fire, he can't be deputized anymore."

"But Ma! Oh, what will Ma and Diana do if Pa doesn't work?" Jacob's ease vanished.

"I'll make sure your Ma and sister are taken care of Jacob," Martin promised.

"But how?" Jacob asked. "Especially with the exchange center burned down. How will they get money to feed themselves and the animals? Diana can't work because she's too busy at home takin' care of Ma."

"How's this for now?" Martin asked. "I'll buy them a week's worth of supplies and try to find another doctor to see your Ma. Then, I'll have a long chat with your Pa about quittin' his drinking, maybe get him to see the errors of his ways so he'll start lookin' for some type of work. I can't promise you he'll change his ways, but I can try. You'll have to await trial, and we've got to find you a good lawyer, too. We'll just take it one step at a time."

"I suppose you're right," Jacob said.

Chapter 19

Jessica came home the next afternoon, her hat pulled low, as if she meant to disappear into it. The wind tugged at her coat, but she didn't seem to notice.

The girls embraced without speaking.

"I heard," Jessica said finally, her voice thin. "Everyone in Boone is talking about the fire. Is it settled?"

Diana pulled back. "Not in the slightest."

Jessica searched her face. "I knew you would say that."

They walked together, their boots striking in unison.

"Papa sent a letter," Jessica went on. "He said Jacob confessed outright. He said it was a mercy Jacob spared Robert worse trouble."

"I'm sorry, Jessica. I know Pastor Howard is your Pa, but that don't sound like mercy to me."

"No," Jessica agreed.

They did not go to the Puckett house. Diana knew better than to bring this weight inside where her mother lay fragile and shaking. Instead, she led Jessica straight toward the jail.

The building squatted low against the road, stone walls cold and unyielding. Diana reached for the door.

"Jessica."

They turned.

Pastor Howard stood at the edge of the street, hat in hand, his expression firm with resolve.

"You won't go in there," he said.

Jessica's shoulders squared.

"Papa, I have a right . . ."

"No," he replied. "You do not."

Diana felt heat rise in her chest. "Sir, Jacob ain't been convicted of anything."

Pastor Howard did not look at her. "That boy's choices have consequences."

"And who decides that?" Jessica demanded.

"I do," he said quietly. "As your father."

He stepped closer to the door, blocking it fully now. Diana noticed how deliberate the move was.

"Papa," Jessica said, her voice breaking. "You're here like you were expectin' us."

Howard did not deny it.

Diana studied him. "Yes, why are you here, Pastor? You ain't the sheriff."

Howard's gaze flickered just for a moment. "I was asked to be."

"By whom?" Diana pressed.

Howard looked at Jessica. "Come home."

Jessica didn't move.

"Papa," she said slowly. "Do you think Jacob is guilty?"

Silence.

The wind stirred the dust of the road at their feet.

"I think," Howard said at last, "that truth is rarely simple, but association with sin has a way of staining even the innocent."

"That ain't an answer," Diana said, feeling defensive of her brother.

"It's the only one I can give," Howard replied.

Jessica turned to Diana, her eyes bright with unshed tears. "He don't think Jacob did it."

Howard's jaw tightened. "That's enough."

She stepped back from the door at last, but her gaze never left it.

As the young women walked away, Diana glanced one more over her shoulder at the jail, and at Pastor Howard who stood watching them outside its door, almost like he was a prison guard.

"They don't want us askin' questions," Diana said.

Jessica nodded. "Then we're askin' the right ones."

Chapter 20

The woods swallowed sound.

That was why they chose it. The holler tucked deep between two ridges where the creek ran low and the trees grew thick enough to hide a man's sins. Smoke rose thin and white through the branches, barely visible against the mountain fog unless one knew precisely where to look for it.

Martin did.

He dismounted his horse without calling out. The men working the moonshine still looked up anyway.

"Well, now," one of them said, wiping his hands on his trousers. "Evenin', Deputy."

Martin dipped his head. "Evenin'."

Copper gleamed in the firelight. The mash bubbled slow and steady, the scent sharp enough to sting the nose. It was good, strong liquor. The kind that dulled memory and sharpened despair.

"I told you to make it stronger," Martin said.

One man grinned. "You won't find stronger this side of Tennessee."

Martin reached down, opened a jar, and took a measured sip. It burned hot and deep. He welcomed it.

"That'll do," he said.

Another man chuckled. "Reckon it helped."

Martin capped the jar. "It did."

The men exchanged looks.

"Shame, though," Martin went on lightly, "that Robert didn't take the blame for the fire."

The grin faded.

"He would've," one man said. "If the boy hadn't stepped in."

"Yes," Martin said. "How noble of him."

He turned his gaze back to the still and watched the fire breathe beneath it. For a fleeting, dangerous moment, he wondered if it might have been better had Robert stayed near the flames that night. Perhaps it would have been better if the drink had dulled him enough that he hadn't stumbled away in time.

A quicker mercy.

At least then the boy wouldn't be sittin' in a cell for his father's failures.

Martin swallowed the thought as easily as the liquor.

"One thing you should know," Martin said. "The county voted dry for a reason. If this comes back to me . . ."

"It won't," one man cut in. "We ain't fools."

Another nodded. "Robert never talked, either. Not once."

Martin raised a brow. "He didn't?"

"No sir," the man said. He covered for us more times than we deserve. He bought steady too, even when the money was tight."

Martin smiled thinly. "Loyalty's a dangerous habit."

The men laughed uneasily.

"Well," one of them said. "We thank him for that."

Martin slipped the jar into his saddlebag. "You'd best."

He mounted his horse and turned away from the glow of the still. The woods closed in again, hiding the fire, the liquor, and the truth.

Chapter 21

Diana had not meant to spy on her friend.

She had only followed Jessica home because she did not want her friend to walk into that house alone.

The Reece parsonage sat quiet beneath the trees, its windows glowing warm against the coming dusk.

Jessica went in through the front door. Diana lingered at the edge of the yard, uncertain, until she noticed the parlor window stood open a few inches, the curtain stirring with the breeze.

She crouched low behind the laurel bush without thinking. The leaves brushed her sleeves, damp and cool, and the earth smelled rich beneath her palms.

Inside, chairs scraped softly.

“Papa,” Jessica said. Her voice was steady, but Diana could hear the strain beneath it. “Why were you really at the jail today?”

There was a pause.

"I was asked to be there," Pastor Howard replied.

"By whom?"

Another pause; longer this time.

Diana leaned closer.

"That don't matter," Howard said. "What matters is that Jacob Puckett has confessed to a crime."

"You know he didn't do it," Jessica said. "I know it. I feel it."

"Feelings aren't proof," Howard replied.

"I don't need proof," Jessica said, her voice breaking at last. "I just need to see him. Just once, so he knows he ain't alone."

"No," Howard said firmly. "Guilty or not, you will stay away from him for the family's sake."

"For whose family?" Jessica asked. "Jacob and Diana's family?"

"Our family," he said. "The church family. This scandal . . ."

"It's not a scandal if he's innocent!"

Howard's voice hardened. "Don't sass me, daughter! Innocence does not erase association."

Diana's stomach twisted.

Jessica drew a shaky breath. "I'm sorry, Papa. I just don't understand how all of this could happen so suddenly . . . or how you so quickly have become friendly with Deputy Martin?"

The name fell like a dropped plate.

Diana held her breath.

Howard cleared his throat. “He is an officer of the law.”

“I mean no disrespect sir, but that ain’t what I asked.”

A chair creaked.

“He came to me for counsel,” Howard said at last. “As men do.”

Jessica did not speak right away. When she did, her voice was quiet. “You’re lying.”

“Jessica!”

“You are,” she insisted. “I know when you are.”

Howard’s reply came too fast. “You’re tired. You’ve been travelin’. You need rest.”

“That doesn’t explain why you stood between me and the jail door,” Jessica said. “That doesn’t explain why you won’t let me see the man I’m promised to.”

“I am protecting you!” Howard insisted.

“No,” Jessica said. “You’re protectin’ somethin’ else.”

The curtain fluttered. Diana pressed herself lower into the bush, her heart pounding.

“Papa,” Jessica said softly, “do you think Jacob deserves this?”

Howard did not answer.

The silence told Diana everything.

At last, Howard spoke. “You will go back to Boone next week. You will finish your schooling. And this will pass.”

Inside, footsteps moved away. A door opened and then closed.

Jessica did not cry.

Diana stayed hidden until the lamp was dimmed and the house settled into stillness. Only then did she rise, legs stiff, breath shallow.

The truth was no longer just twisted.

It was being guarded.

Diana knew then, without a doubt, that whatever lay beneath it was dangerous enough to silence a pastor.

She slipped back into the dark, carrying what she’d heard like a live coal pressed to her chest.

Chapter 22

Deputy Martin made sure to be present.

He stood near the desk when the Puckett women arrived, hat removed out of courtesy, and with a posture loose enough to feign kindness.

Margaret Puckett leaned heavily on her daughter, her body betraying her before her mouth ever could. The disease was winning. Everyone could see it.

"Mrs. Puckett," Martin said gently. "Diana."

Diana acknowledged him with a nod that carried no warmth.

Jacob rose the moment he saw them. Hope crossed his face. Martin cleared his throat, not loudly, but just enough that the boy would notice.

"Ma," Jacob said, softening. "You shouldn't have come."

"I had to," Margaret whispered, gripping the bars. 'I had to hear it from you."

Martin watched Jacob choose each word as if weighing them on a scale.

"Tell us what happened," Diana said.

Jacob glanced at Martin. Just a flick of the eyes. Good. The boy was learning.

"There ain't much to tell," Jacob said. "It was an accident."

Diana frowned. "You told me differently.

Jacob swallowed. "I said what needed sayin' at the time."

Martin stepped closer. "You're doin' right, son."

Jacob nodded.

After a moment, Jacob said, "I need a lawyer."

Diana stiffened. "What?"

"There's a good one in Boone," Jacob continued, careful now. "I heard folks say so."

Margaret's face fell. "Boone?" she whispered. "We can't afford a lawyer."

Martin watched the hope drain from her eyes.

Margaret turned to him then, her desperation spilling over. "Deputy Martin," she pleaded, "you've known our family a long time. Please help us."

Martin met her gaze steadily. "I'll see what I can do."

Diana did not believe him. He could tell by the way she squared her shoulders and the way her eyes sharpened instead of softened.

"Thank you," Margaret whispered.

Martin nodded. "It's my duty."

The visit ended soon after. Jacob pressed his hand against the bars as his family turned to leave.

Martin watched the women leave. The daughter was stiff with suspicion.

When the door closed behind them, the jail settled back into its familiar quiet.

Martin straightened his coat.

A lawyer from Boone would complicate matters.

Chapter 23

A week passed, as slow and heavy as a held breath.

Sunday came again, cool and bright, the mountains dressed in early autumn colors. The church service ended as it always did, with the scrape of pew benches, the low murmur of voices, and the bell's hollow echo rolling out across the hills.

Diana lingered near the maple tree, watching folks speak to one another as if nothing had changed. As if a good man weren't still sitting behind iron bars.

Jessica joined her, folding her hands in front of her like she was still in the pew. "Papa'll allow it," she said quietly. "He won't make a scene about us talkin' to each other with everyone watchin'."

Diana studied her face. "You sound sure."

"I am," Jessica replied. "Appearances matter too much to him."

They stood a moment, the breeze stirring fallen leaves at their feet

“There’s something I need to tell you,” Diana said. Her voiced stayed low. “I heard what you and Pastor Howard said at your house the other night.”

Jessica turned to her, eyes widening just slightly. “You heard?”

“I didn’t mean to,” Diana said quickly. “But the window was open, and . . . I needed to know.”

Jessica’s expression softened. “Then you know.”

“I do,” Diana said. “And I know this too: Jacob needs a lawyer. A good one from Boone.”

Jessica nodded.

“The deputy said he’d help with the money,” Diana added. “But I don’t trust him.”

“Neither do I,” Jessica said without hesitation.

They watched Pastor Howard speaking with two elders near the steps, his face composed, his gestures measured.

“No one suspects me of anything when I’m in Boone,” Jessica said slowly. “I’m just a student there.”

Diana’s heart lifted. “What are you thinkin’?”

“I’ll take in laundry,” Jessica said. “From the girls in my dormitory. I’ll wash it in the evening. I can raise enough if I am careful.”

Diana reached for her hand. “That’s a lot to take on.”

“So is watchin’ the man you love rot in a cell,” Jessica replied.

"And when you've got the money?" Diana asked.

Jessica's eyes burned with determination "I'll go see the lawyer myself while I'm there. No one will think twice about it."

Diana squeezed her hand. "You're braver than you know."

Jessica shook her head. "I'm just tired of waitin' for permission."

The bell rang out again, and the congregation thinned as people began to head home.

For the first time in days, Diana felt something shift—not the lifting of the burden, but of sharing it with a trusted sister in Christ who wanted to do what was right.

Chapter 24

Robert Puckett swung first.

Martin had expected anger, resentment, and even tears, but not the sudden, desperate violence that exploded out of the man like a cork pulled too fast. The blow caught Martin across the jaw, glancing more than solid, but hard enough to send him staggering back against the fence.

"Don't you speak her name," Robert snarled.

Martin wiped blood from his lip with the back of his hand and laughed softly. "You always were quick to anger."

Robert lunged again. This time, Martin caught his arm, twisting it just enough to throw him off balance. They crashed into the dirt together, with their boots scraping and fists flying into a clumsy, graceless tangle of rage and years-old resentment.

Robert was stronger than he looked when he was sober. Martin had forgotten that.

They rolled apart, breathing hard.

"You come to shame me now?" Robert barked. "After everything?"

"I came to tell you the truth," Martin said evenly, though his jaw throbbed. "Your wife asked me for help."

Robert froze.

"Margaret came to me," Martin continued as he brushed dirt from his coat. "She asked about a lawyer for Jacob. I figured she asked me because you can't manage it. Everyone knows the money is gone as soon as it comes in."

Robert's face flushed deep red. "You had no right."

"She's afraid," Martin said. "And she had every right to be. You've left her with nothin' but worry and sickness."

Robert swung again, but his strength was gone now. Martin stepped aside easily, letting Robert stumble forward.

"You don't get to judge me," Robert shouted. "Not you. You're the one who put that bottle in my hand."

Martin smiled and shrugged his shoulders. "I offered. You drank."

"You showed me how," Robert said hoarsely. "You brought it to me after the doctor told us she wouldn't get better. You said it would help me to sleep and help me to forget."

Martin shrugged. "And it did."

“For a while.” Robert’s voice broke. “Then it took everything else. You let my boy take the fall,” Robert said, his words thick with shame. “You let him.”

Martin met his gaze without flinching. “Your boy stepped forward.”

“Because I wouldn’t,” Robert spat.

Martin lowered his voice. “Then perhaps this is the price of that failure.”

Robert sank against the fence post, head in his hands. The fight had drained out of him, leaving only the wreckage behind.

“You think you’re savin’ my family?” Robert whispered. “You’re just spreadin’ the hurt around so it don’t land on you.”

Martin adjusted his coat. “I’m keepin’ order.”

Robert looked up, eyes red and burning. “No, you’re burying us.”

Martin stepped back, giving him space, even as he knew Robert would never climb out of it.

Martin touched his bruised jaw and smiled thinly.

Some men drank to forget.

Others remembered everything and chose power instead.

Chapter 25

Diana saw the fight from the yard.

She had been hanging out clothes behind the house when raised voices cut through the afternoon air. She rounded the corner just in time to see her father lunge, his fist catching Deputy Martin square across the jaw. The sound carried, sharp and ugly, followed by the dull thud of bodies hitting the ground.

Her heart seized.

By the time she reached the fence, the men had already broken apart. Martin straightened his coat, blood at the corner of his mouth, and said something low that she couldn't hear. Then he walked away without looking back.

"Pa," Diana whispered, running to her father.

Robert swayed on his feet, his face pale beneath the grime. "I'm all right," he muttered.

"Come on," she said, slipping her arm around his waist. "Let's get you inside."

She guided him through the door as gently as she could. The cabin was quiet. Margaret lay in the back room resting.

"Keep your voice down," Diana whispered. "Ma's sleepin'."

Robert nodded, letting himself be eased into a chair. Blood trickled from his split lip, and a bruise was already blooming along his cheekbone. Diana fetched a cloth and a basin, kneeling in front of him.

As she cleaned the cut, she said softly, "Pa, can you tell me what really happened the night of the fire?"

Robert stared at his hands. "The truth is," he said after a moment, "I ain't real clear on it."

Diana had expected as much.

"I'd been drinkin' at the Green Park Inn," he continued. "More than I ought to. Jacob came to fetch me home. He said your ma would be worryin' because it was so late. He tried to get me to leave."

"And you wouldn't go," Diana guessed.

Robert shook his head. "I wouldn't budge."

He swallowed hard. "Next thing I remember, there was fire. I was no longer at the inn. I was behind the businesses on Main Street. Smoke was everywhere, and I don't know how I got there."

Diana's hands stilled.

"I woke up on the ground," Robert said, his voice rough. "The fire was smoldering, and then," his voice broke, "Jacob was takin' the blame."

"I don't think you started the fire either, Pa," Diana said firmly.

Robert shook his head. "I don't remember startin' it, and I don't think I would have. I know I was drunk, but I ain't no fool. I think . . ." He looked up at her, eyes wet. "I think I was framed."

"I think so too," Diana said.

She finished dressing his wounds and sat back on her heels. "Pa, you've got to stop drinkin'."

"I know," he whispered. "God help me, I know. The sheriff fired me." He burst into tears.

"Alright, the sheriff fired you," she repeated. "But that don't mean you're done. It don't mean you can't still be my Pa, and my mother's husband."

Robert covered his face with his hands. "I don't know how to do right anymore."

"We'll figure it out," Diana said. "Jessica's raisin' money for a lawyer in Boone. We're keepin' it quiet for now."

Robert looked up. "That girl's got more courage than most men."

"Yes, sir," Diana chuckled, proud of her friend and future sister-in-law.

"Di," Robert said. "Would you pray for your old Pa?"

Her throat tightened. "Of course."

They bowed their heads there in the kitchen.

"Lord," Diana prayed. "You see us. You see all the wrong that's been done and all the hurt that's come of it. Give us the truth. Give us strength. And please, please, please, bring my brother home."

Robert added, "Forgive me, and please help me do better than I've done."

When they lifted their heads, the room around them hadn't changed, except now, there was hope.

Chapter 26

Deputy Martin was sorting papers in the sheriff's office when Pastor Howard Reece appeared in the doorway.

"Deputy," Howard said. "Have you a moment?"

Martin looked up at him. "For you, Pastor, I always have a moment."

Howard stepped inside and closed the door behind him. "I ran into Robert Puckett this mornin'."

Martin's pen paused.

"And?" he asked.

"He asked after his boy," Howard continued. "I told him Jacob was holdin' up as well as could be expected."

Martin leaned back in his chair to listen.

Pastor Howard shifted his weight. "I mentioned, only in passing, that I'd heard help was comin'. That you were seein' about getting Jacob a lawyer."

"Who told you that?" he asked.

Howard hesitated. "Jessica heard it from Diana."

Martin stood. That was the trouble with Blowing Rock. Nothing stayed private for long. Words traveled the way smoke did, slipping through the cracks, carried on breath and assumption until they reached the wrong ears.

"That wasn't the arrangement," he said quietly.

Howard frowned. "I thought . . .?"

"You were told," Martin interrupted, "to put an end to all communication between your daughter and the Puckett family."

Howard stiffened. "I told her to keep away from Jacob."

"And I meant the whole of them," Martin said.

Howard swallowed, "The Puckett girl has been her best friend since they were very young. It will be difficult to make her give up a long friendship. She's strong willed."

"That can be corrected," Martin replied.

He stepped closer now. "Boone is a fine place for a young woman. Reputations are built there, but they can be lost there, too. You know, as a deputy, I serve the whole of the county, not just Blowing Rock, and I know from being there, that a single suggestion in the wrong ear . . . like an accusation of impropriety or of disobedience . . . can undo years of careful raisin'."

Howard's face was drained of color. "You wouldn't."

"I wouldn't need to," Martin said. "People draw their own conclusions."

Howard stared at the floor.

"Remember, Pastor. Your daughter's future depends on restraint," Martin went on. "So does Jacob Puckett's future. If Jessica keeps meddlin', folks might begin to wonder why, and wonderin' has consequences."

Howard looked up sharply. "You're threatenin' my child."

"I'm advisin' her father as a man of law," Martin retorted.

Pastor Howard said nothing.

"See that she returns to Boone and stays there," Martin said.

Howard nodded, stiffly.

When he left, Martin returned to the desk and sat heavily. Anger simmered just beneath his skin.

The Puckett girl was moving faster than he'd expected.

That would have to be addressed.

Chapter 27

Pa came in from the yard just after supper, his shoulders slumped.

"I went lookin'," he said without preamble.

Diana set aside the dish she was drying. "Find anything?"

He shook his head. "Nobody'll hire me even though I'm sober."

Her heart sank. "Pa . . ."

"They don't trust me," he went on. "I can't say I blame them."

He sat at the table and rubbed his hands together, the way he used to when he was thinking hard. "The only work I can get is out in the woods."

"Moonshine?" Diana asked.

He nodded.

"Pa, that's dangerous," she said. "Martin already knows about that operation, and if you're around drink . . ."

"I know," Robert said quietly. "It's dangerous for a lot of reasons, but I don't have another choice."

Diana swallowed. "Ma can't know."

"I won't tell her," he said. "And neither will you."

She nodded, though the weight of keeping such a secret from her mother settled heavy in her stomach.

"I'm trying, Di," he added. "I truly am."

"I know," Diana said.

***

Later that night, Diana sat at the table and pulled out paper and pen, and the ink bottle still half-full.

Dear Jessica, she wrote.

She told Jessica everything she could without saying too much. She wrote about Pa staying sober, about his fear, about how proud she was of him even when the road ahead felt crooked and unclear. She asked about the laundry money and whether it was adding up yet.

Pa stoppin' the drink feels like an answered prayer, she wrote. *I'm holdin' onto that.*

She folded the letter carefully and set it by the door.

Her mother stirred, emerging from the bedroom with sleep still clinging to her features.

"I've been thinkin'," Margaret said, "Would you like to go into town tomorrow to see Jacob? Maybe we can find out when his court date might be."

Diana smiled. "I'd like that." She'd post the letter while they were in town.

Chapter 28

Martin noticed them the moment they crossed the street.

From the sheriff's office window, he watched Diana peel away toward the post office, her stride purposeful, while Margaret lingered, speaking with Mrs. Lentz. Margaret looked frailer than the last time he'd seen her. She was too thin and too pale.

Martin took his hat from the peg and stepped outside.

He crossed the street just as Diana disappeared through the post office door. Mrs. Lentz turned at his approach, surprise on her face.

"Mrs. Puckett," Martin said warmly, tipping his hat. "I was hopin' to speak with you."

Mrs. Lentz smiled. "Of course, Deputy Martin." She glanced between them, then took the hint. "I'll leave you to it."

She moved quickly, curiosity already pulling her steps away.

Martin turned back to Margaret. "You shouldn't be standin' so long," he said. "Your health . . ."

"I'm fine, I assure you," Margaret replied. "The walking is good for me. What can I do for you Deputy? Is this about Jacob?"

"I want to speak plainly," Martin ventured. "Not about Jacob, but about Robert."

Margaret stiffened. "What about him?"

"No one would fault you," Martin said carefully, "if you choose to leave him."

Her brow furrowed. "Leave him?"

"He's been dismissed from the sheriff's office," Martin continued. "Quietly, of course."

The color drained from Margaret's face. "That isn't possible," she said. "Robert goes to work every day."

Martin shook his head slowly. "I'm sorry you weren't told. It seems your husband was hiding it from you."

Margaret's hand trembled as she gripped the edge of a post used by locals to tie horses while they went shopping.

"He's stopped drinkin'," she said firmly. "He's doin' better."

Martin lowered his voice. "I have undercover connections. They're men who help funnel out moonshinin' operations in the county."

Her eyes widened.

"Robert's still involved," Martin said. "He's still around the liquor. That alone should tell you he ain't fit to care for you."

"That's a lie," Margaret said defiantly.

"It's proof," Martin replied. "No one would fault you if you secured a divorce. You could begin again, this time with a man who would see to you properly in every way."

Margaret straightened then, slowly, seemingly painfully, but unmistakably.

"Deputy Martin," she said steadily, "you have been a friend to my family for a long time."

He nodded.

"And that is the only reason I will speak kindly now," she went on. "You are oversteppin' bounds. You are bein' disrespectful. And I thank you for your concern, but I will not hear another word of it."

She moved to pass him.

Martin stepped aside instinctively, then felt the eyes on him. They were the storekeepers, passersby, and men pausing mid-conversation. There were too many witnesses.

Margaret pushed past him and mounted the steps to the sheriff's office.

"This conversation is over," she said without turning back. "I'm here to see my son."

Martin followed, his pulse quickening.

She opened the door.

"Where is my son?" Margaret asked.

Martin turned toward the cell.

And froze.

The bench was empty. The bars stood open, and the space Jacob Puckett should have filled was vacant.

Deputy Martin felt the ground shift beneath his feet.

Jacob Puckett was gone.

Chapter 29

Diana stepped out of the post office and began looking around for her mother.

Mrs. Lentz stood nearby, twisting her gloves. “Your ma just went into the sheriff’s office with Deputy Martin,” she said.

Diana hurried across the street, the sounds of town blurring around her. As she climbed the steps, she could hear raised voices spilling through the door.

“Where is he?” her mother cried. “Where is my son?”

“I don’t know,” Martin snapped back, “but he didn’t leave on his own.”

The sheriff’s office was chaotic with papers strewn and a chair overturned, likely where Martin had thrown them in his anger. Margaret stood in the center of the room, one hand braced against the desk, her breathing ragged, her face ashen.

“Ma!” Diana ran to her side.

Before Margaret could tell her daughter what had happened, the sheriff himself came through the door.

"What's all this?" Sheriff Critcher demanded.

Martin spoke first. "The boy's gone."

Sheriff Critcher turned sharply toward the cell. "He escaped?"

Martin nodded. "It looks like he had help. The bars weren't forced. The door was opened careful-like."

Diana's chest tightened.

"Who?" the sheriff asked.

Martin didn't hesitate. "It had to have been Robert Puckett."

"No!" Diana shouted. "That ain't true!"

Margaret cried out, clutching Diana's arm. "Robert wouldn't do that!"

The sheriff frowned. "Where's Robert now?"

Diana answered, "He is at work!"

Martin seized on it. "He's moonshinin'. That's where he's been spendin' his time."

Margaret swayed. Diana caught her just in time.

"Spread the word," the sheriff ordered. Tell the Blowing Rock Police. Get men out on the ridge paths, the hollers, and the road toward Boone."

"They'll kill him," Margaret sobbed. "They'll think he's guilty. They'll hunt my husband and son like animals."

Diana held her mother, rocking her gently. "Ma, breathe. Please."

Margaret was inconsolable, her words tumbling over one another.

Diana looked around the room at the men arming themselves. This wasn't justice. It was a witch hunt.

"We need to go home," Diana said to her mother. "You need rest."

"I can't leave," Margaret cried. "Jacob and Robert need me."

"I'll find Jacob," Diana promised, though fear clawed at her throat. "But your staying here won't do them any good."

With help from Mrs. Lentz and another woman, Diana guided her mother back to their wagon. They watched as men mounted horses and grabbed their rifles.

As they turned toward home, Diana looked back once, at the sheriff's office and at Martin pointing his fingers as he issued orders for Jacob's and Robert's arrests.

Diana never saw Jacob's disappearance coming.

Chapter 30

The woods went quiet when the horses came.

"Law," someone muttered.

"Show yourself," Martin called out.

Men stepped out of the dark.

"What's goin' on here?" one of them demanded from Martin as they looked around him at the other lawmen that accompanied him

"Easy now," Martin said as he spat into the dirt.

"Jacob Puckett has gone missing from the jail," one Blowing Rock policeman said. "And now we find all of this," he said as he briefly nodded his rifle toward the still.

The men at the moonshine still shifted nervously.

Martin stopped forward. "They're with me."

That gave the policemen pause.

"They're my . . . undercover contacts," Martin said, forcing the words steady. "The sheriff knows about it. I was helpin' funnel out moonshine."

This was a lie, but close enough to the truth to pass.

The policemen exchanged looks. One of them scoffed. "Since when do you get put on that kind of work in Blowing Rock? This is our jurisdiction."

Martin looked at the man angrily. "The whole of the county is my jurisdiction."

Silence fell heavier than before.

"Has Robert been here recently?" Martin asked the moonshiners.

One of the men nodded his head. "He was earlier, but then he left. He said he had somethin' to tend to."

"He did?" Martin prompted for more information.

"Yes," the man said. "He didn't say where he was agoin'."

The deputy's eyes sharpened. The policemen exchanged looks.

"Sounds like you got somethin' to hide," one of them said.

"They're tellin' the truth. Come on, boys. Let's go," he said to the policemen.

They turned back toward town, leaving the moonshiners standing still, exchanging grim looks with one another.

"Ain't this proof that the boy's Pa helped him escape?" one of the officers asked.

"Seems to be pointin' that way." Martin smiled.

Chapter 31

It took longer than it should have to get Ma to lie down.

Margaret's hands trembled even after the blankets were pulled up, her eyes darting about as though Jacob might step through the door at any moment. Diana sat on the edge of the bed and brushed her mother's hair back from her forehead, humming softly.

"Try to rest, Ma," Diana whispered. "I'll be right here."

Margaret's eyes finally closed.

Only then did Diana let herself breathe.

She stepped out onto the porch and folded her hands tight, the mountains dark against the evening sky.

"Lord," she prayed, *"keep my pa safe. Keep him from harm and from men who already think the worst of him. And wherever Jacob is, don't let him be alone."*

I need to start at the beginning, she thought to herself.

Diana fetched a shawl, and her Pa's pistol for safety. She walked the long road into town, her steps steady, even when her thoughts were not.

The Green Park Inn glowed warm against the night. Lanterns were lit and laughter drifted through the windows. It felt wrong that the world could keep moving when her brother was missing.

She pushed open the door.

The smell of tobacco met her nose. Behind the bar, stood Mr. Miller, polishing a glass with slow, practiced motions. He looked up and stiffened when he saw her.

"Well," he said carefully. "If it ain't Miss Puckett. I don't think you should be here unchaperoned so late at night, little lady."

"I know," Diana said, "but it's important. I need to ask you somethin' about the night my Pa was here. The night of the fire."

Miller glanced around, then nodded toward the far end of the bar. "Come on."

They stood where the shadows were thickest.

"My pa was drinkin' that night," Diana said. "I know that. And I know that Jacob came to get him."

"That's right," Miller said. "Your brother tried hard, too, but he was respectful. He kept sayin', 'Pa, Ma needs you.'"

Diana swallowed. That sounded just like something Jacob would say. "Did my Pa or brother start any trouble?"

"No," Miller said firmly. "Not once. Your pa didn't raise his voice. He didn't touch nothin'. Jacob just stood there waitin'."

"What did my Pa say about going home?" she asked.

Martin sighed. "Robert was stubborn. He wouldn't budge. He said he could handle himself."

"Did he leave with Jacob?"

"No," Miller said. "At least, not at first."

"Then what happened?" Diana asked.

"Deputy Martin came in. He told Jacob he needed help with a call. Robert stumbled up then, said he ought to see what was goin' on. Jacob followed him out, keepin' close."

"Did my Pa or brother ever come back inside after that?"

Miller shook his head. "No ma'am. They never came back in."

Diana pressed her hands together thinking about what she should ask next. "Did you see anyone else actin' strange?"

Miller hesitated.

"Maybe Martin," he said finally. "He actually came through earlier that night. He didn't drink much. He just watched. He asked me a lot of questions about how

I manage the bar now that the referendum has banned the sale of alcohol."

Diana felt a chill.

"Thank you," she said softly.

As she turned to leave, Mr. Miller called after her. "Miss Puckett, Jacob ain't no arsonist, and if the law's sayin' otherwise, they're wrong."

She stepped back into the night, thankful that at least one person supported Jacob.

Chapter 32

Martin was furious.

Not the hot kind that burned off quick, but the cold kind that sat behind his eyes and made everything feel sharp.

Robert should have been there.

The moonshiners had said it plain enough. Robert left early. He had slipped off before the law could come sniff. Martin had counted on finding him among the barrels and copper coils where he could drag him in with proof enough to finish him for good.

Instead, Robert Puckett was still free.

Martin rode his horse around without thinking, the road curling upward until the trees thinned and the sky opened wide. He stopped near the edge of the Blowing Rock, the town's namesake. The wind rose immediately, tugging at his coat. Winter was coming soon.

He stepped out and walked toward the overlook.

The sun was sinking low, staining the mountains red and gold instead of blue. It was the kind of beauty that made men quiet and sometimes made them retrospectively think of things they didn't want to.

Martin took out his flask.

The first swallow burned. The second settled.

His Pa had told him the story when he was a boy.

A Chickasaw chief detested a white man's interest in his daughter, so he left the plains for the mountains, and hid her atop the high cliff. One day, the young woman spied a Cherokee man in the wilderness below her mountain top and she shot an arrow at him to get his attention.

The Cherokee man climbed up to see her and fell in love with her. One day, the sky was red, much like on this night, Martin thought. The Cherokee man told the Chickasaw woman that the color of the sky was a sign that he should return to his people. She was sad. Her father had commanded her to stay, but she loved the Cherokee man. She didn't want him to go and begged him not to leave her.

Torn between his love for this woman and his duty to his people, he leaped off the rock into the night. The woman was distraught at this loss of her love. She fell to her knees, praying that by some miracle he might return to her.

A miracle was gifted. Suddenly, the harsh winds blew the man back up on the rock. It was a sign that the two would be together, and they lived happily ever after. This is how the rock cliff became known as the Blowing Rock.

Martin stared over the edge. Funny how stories softened over time. How folks preferred happy, pretty endings to real life.

He drank again.

People talked about Blowing Rock like it was a place for miracles, like it was a place where wrongs were lifted away if you stepped out enough. Martin snorted softly.

He had stepped out plenty far already.

Behind him, the wind howled through the rocks, rising and falling like a voice that wouldn't quite speak.

He told himself he wasn't the villain. That he was cleaning up a mess that should have been handled years ago. That if Robert had been a better husband, a better father, none of this would have happened.

The flask was nearly empty.

Martin wiped his mouth and looked once more into the darkening valley. The sun dipped below the ridge. Martin stayed where he was, alone with the story he'd chosen to believe.

Chapter 33

Diana woke to the sound of hooves.

It was a slow, deliberate rhythm on the packed dirt road, the kind that belonged to a man who knew he would be received. She sat up at once, pulling her shawl around her shoulders, and peered out the window.

Pastor Howard Reece sat straight-backed on his horse.

Her stomach tightened.

She helped her mother from bed and eased her into the rocker near the window before stepping out onto the porch.

“Mornin’, Pastor,” Diana said.

“Good mornin’, Diana,” he replied. “May I speak with you and your mother?”

Margaret nodded weakly, and Diana ushered him inside.

Pastor Howard did not sit.

"I came because Robert Puckett came to see me yesterday," he said gently. "He wished to confess his sins."

Diana gasped.

"He told me," Pastor Howard continued, "that he intends to turn himself in for the fire."

The words settled heavily in the room.

Diana found her voice. "Did my pa say he started the fire?"

Pastor Howard hesitated only a moment. "Yes."

Diana nodded slowly, though her thoughts raced. *Pa told me he didn't remember starting it. He said he wasn't sure how he got there at all.*

Margaret clutched the arm of her chair. "Did he say . . . did he say he helped Jacob escape?"

"No," Pastor Howard said firmly. "I do not believe Robert would have done such a thing. He knows the state of his standing with the sheriff. He would not have gone near the jail, certainly not with Deputy Martin watchin'. Shame keeps men away from places where they once belonged."

Margaret sagged back into her chair, tears spilling freely now. "Then Jacob's still out there . . . alone."

"I will take you into town," Pastor Howard said. "You ought to see Robert and hear it from him yourself."

Diana reached for her mother's hand.

As Pastor Howard stepped back onto the porch, Diana glanced toward the mountains, wondering where her brother could be.

She knew deep in her bones that not all confessions were born of guilt.

Some were born of love.

Chapter 34

Pastor Howard's buggy rolled up slow and proper, the horse blowing from the climb. Diana climbed down first, careful with her mother, one hand firm at Margaret's elbow.

So, Howard had brought them himself.

He waited until the women disappeared inside the sheriff's office before stepping forward.

"You had no business bringin' them here," Martin said, low and sharp.

Pastor Howard turned to face him, calm as ever. "I had every business. They deserve to know Robert confessed to me before turnin' himself in."

"That wasn't your place," Martin snapped. "I told you to keep your distance from the Pucketts."

Howard's brows drew together. "You told me to keep my daughter away from them. You don't get to dictate who I minister to."

Martin scoffed. “You’re skirtin’ the line, Pastor.”

Howard met his gaze squarely. “I will not avoid my congregants because it makes you more comfortable.”

“Robert Puckett is poisonous, and those women, whether you like it or not, they’re part of his mess.”

Howard folded his hands. “They are frightened and hurting. They trust their minister.”

Martin’s eyes flashed toward the door. “Trust gets folks in trouble.”

Something clicked in Martin’s mind then, sharp and sudden.

Boone.

Jessica.

He straightened. “That boy didn’t just disappear.”

Howard said nothing.

“Jacob’s smart,” Martin continued. “And desperate. The only place he’d run is somewhere he thought he had help.”

Howard’s lips pressed thin.

“Boone,” Martin said aloud. “Perhaps Appalachian State Normal School, where your daughter is.”

Howard stiffened. “You best be careful.”

“If Jessica’s hiding him,” Martin said coldly, “she’ll be implicated. Same as anyone else who helped.

Howard stopped closer. “How dare you!”

“I’m just statin’ the facts,” Martin said. “I’m goin’ to Boone to see for myself.”

Howard didn't hesitate. “Then I’m comin’ with you.”

Martin barked a short laugh. “This ain’t your affair.”

“It became my affair when you started usin’ my daughter’s name as leverage,” Howard replied. “And when you forget justice ain’t yours to bend.”

Martin looked once more at the sheriff’s office door, then back at the pastor.

“Fine,” he said. “But don’t expect me to soften.”

Howard mounted his horse and buggy to wait to take the women home. “I wouldn’t expect anything less.”

If Jacob was in Boone, this would end soon.

And if he wasn’t . . .

Martin clenched his jaw.

Then someone would pay for making him look like a fool.

Chapter 35

The jail felt smaller than it had before. Diana stood close to her pa's cell while her mother hovered near the door, wringing her hands.

"Robert," Margaret whispered. "You didn't . . . you didn't let Jacob out, did you?"

Robert shook his head at once. "No, Maggie. I swear it. I wouldn't risk that. Not for nothin'. I didn't even know he was gone till I came to confess."

Margaret pressed her hand to her chest. "We can't afford lawyers for both of you."

Robert bowed his head. "I know."

Tears slipped free then, and Margaret turned away, her shoulders trembling. "I need some air," she said faintly.

Diana guided her mother outside and settled her on the steps, the sounds of Martin and Pastor Howard's raised voices drifting from around the corner. Diana slipped back inside.

She stepped closer to the bars.

Pa," she said. "I went to the Green Park Inn last night."

"You shouldn't have. That's no place for a young lady unchaperoned in the dark."

"I had to," Diana continued. "I talked to Mr. Miller. He said Jacob tried to take you home. He said Martin was there, too, earlier, asking him all sorts of questions about the drinks."

Robert exhaled slow. "That matches what I remember. Except for Martin being there. I don't remember that."

"I'm trying to get the facts straight," Diana said. "I want to prove you and Jacob are innocent. Who else should I talk to?"

"There ain't anyone else," Robert said. "No one is going to help you."

Diana's chest tightened. "Pa, there's got to be! Even Mr. Miller said he didn't believe Jacob started that fire."

"There ain't," he repeated. "Especially to help me. Anyone who knows somethin' won't say it. Not with Martin breathin' down their necks."

The weight of his words pressed hard against her ribs.

"Pa, do you think Martin framed you?" she asked quietly, but before Robert couldn't answer, the front door slammed. Diana turned to see Deputy Martin himself, red as a beet and fuming.

She nodded once at her father. "All right. Bye, Pa. I love you."

"I love you too, Di," he said.

Diana brushed past Martin on her way out the door. "*Lord,*" she prayed silently, "*go with me. I want to figure this out.*"

Part 3

The Truth Revealed

"The Lord will perfect that which concerneth me: thy mercy, O LORD, endureth for ever: forsake not the works of thine own hands."
–Psalm 138:8

Chapter 36

The road to Boone wound narrow and uneven. Pastor Howard and Deputy Martin rode alongside one another.

Silence, Martin had learned, was a preacher's weapon.

"You've got a lot to answer for," Howard said at last, his eyes fixed ahead as he spoke.

Martin snorted. "I'm just doin' my job."

"You're doin' damage," Howard replied. "And what's worse is you know it."

Martin shot him a glance. "You didn't seem so troubled when Robert confessed his sins to you."

"Robert confessed more than you know," Howard admitted. "He told me how the drink started and how it worsened.

Martin laughed once, short and sharp. "You gonna blame that on me too?"

“I am,” Howard said plainly. “He told me you were the one who brought him into it. You offered him the first drink. Then, one night of drinking turned into many.”

Martin’s grip tightened on the reins. “Robert is a grown man.”

“So are you,” Howard said. “Yet here you are.”

Howard reached into his coat and pulled out his Bible, holding it between them. “Proverbs 20:1 says, ‘Wine is a mocker, strong drink is raging: and whosoever is deceived thereby is not wise.’”

Martin rolled his eyes. “I don’t get drunk.”

Howard didn’t look at him. “You don’t have to be drunk to be deceived.”

The wind kicked up, snapping at their coats. Martin waited until Howard’s attention was forward before slipping the flask from his pocket and taking a quick swallow. Just enough to steady himself.

Howard saw it anyway.

“You deny the bottle, yet you carry it like a companion,” Howard noted.

Martin wiped his mouth. “It’s for the cold.”

Howard turned toward him. “Isaiah 5:11 says, ‘Woe unto them that rise up early in the morning, that they may follow strong drink, that continue until night, till wine inflame them!’”

Martin bristled. “You done preachin’?”

Howard shook his head. “You think you’re above ruin because you still stand upright.”

Martin laughed again. “Robert chose his path. I chose mine.”

“You nudged him down the path,” Howard repeated. “Then you condemned him for fallin’.”

They rode on in tense silence after that, watching Boone’s distant ridge rising up ahead.

Martin took another swallow when Howard wasn’t looking.

He told himself it didn’t count. He told himself a lot of things.

Chapter 37

The Green Park Inn looked different in the daylight. Without the lantern glow and evening laughter, it felt smaller. Sunlight slated through the front windows, catching dust in the air and settling on the worn wood check-in desk.

Diana paused at the threshold, smoothed her skirt, and stepped inside.

Mr. Miller stood behind the counter, wiping it down with a rag. He looked up and gave a slow nod.

"Mornin', Miss Puckett."

"Mornin, sir," Diana said. "I hope I ain't botherin' you."

He shook his head. "Not at all."

"I was hopin' you might help me understand somethin'. Your information was incredibly helpful the other night, but it's made me think of more questions.

Miller chuckled. "I'll do what I can."

"The night of the fire, my Pa was drinkin' here. Same as usual," she recapped.

Miller nodded to confirm. "Yes, ma'am."

"Is it possible," she asked carefully, "that someone could've tampered with his drink?"

Miller sighed as he thought and leaned his weight on the counter.

"Maybe, but he ordered the same drink as always."

"And who poured it? Was it you?"

"Depends," Miller said. "It was a busy night. Sometimes I do. Sometimes Mr. Lentz does."

"Could anyone else have had access?" Diana pressed.

Miller hesitated, then nodded once. "Deputy Martin's got a habit of wanderin' behind the bar when he's here. He's the law, so folks don't stop him."

"And he was there earlier that day!" Diana gasped. "So, it is possible! Did you see him near my pa's drink?"

Miller rubbed his jaw. "I can't swear to it, but I think I saw him set somethin' down beside our stash. I thought nothin' of it at the time."

Diana swallowed, "So, it could have been stronger than usual?"

Miller's eyes met hers. "It could've been."

"Would that make a man lose time and forget where he'd been?" she asked.

"Of course." Miller nodded.

Diana felt both relief and dread.

"Thank you," she said.

As she turned to leave, Miller spoke again. "Miss Puckett, if I were you, I'd be careful who you let know you're asking these questions."

"I reckon I'm being more than careful," she insisted, as she left the building. Someone had wanted to ensure her Pa was confused the night of the fire. She was betting on Deputy Martin.

Chapter 38

The Appalachian Training School sat high and proud, the brick and white trim standing out too cleanly against the rough country that fed it. Martin reined in beside Pastor Howard and took it all in with narrowed eyes.

They dismounted near the walk just as Jessica stepped out of her dorm building, her books clutched to her chest. Her smile faltered the instant she saw them.

"Papa?" she said. "What's happened?"

Martin watched her face closely as Pastor Howard dismounted. Shock passed through her features as real and unguarded. She was a good actress.

"There's trouble in Blowing Rock," Howard said gently. "Jacob is missin'."

Jessica's breath caught. "Missin'?" She shook his head in disbelief. "Where could he be?"

"We thought you might know. Have you seen or heard from him?" Howard asked his daughter.

"No, I haven't seen him, and I haven't heard a word. Our letters ceased once he was jailed."

Martin stepped forward. "You sure about that?"

Her eyes snapped to his. "I'm telling the truth, Deputy."

Before Martin could press further, a young woman hurried up, her cheeks flushed with the cold. "Jessica, are you still takin' in laundry for your beau's lawyer . . ."

Martin's mouth curved as he interrupted. "Well now," he said. "It seems like you've been raisin' Jacob a secret fund."

Jessica stiffened. "I've been takin' in laundry to pay for his lawyer. That's honest work."

"Work meant to help a fugitive?" Martin shot back.

"That's enough," Pastor Howard said sharply.

Martin turned on him. "Your daughter's been raisin' money under your nose."

Howard did not flinch. "If that is her greatest sin, then I thank God for it. She worked honestly to help the man she loves. There's no crime in that."

Martin scoffed. "It makes her complicit."

"It makes her faithful," Pastor Howard replied. "Your accusations against my daughter end here, Deputy.

Martin wrung his hands together in frustration. "I'm going to the train depot. If Jacob ran, someone saw him leave."

"You do that," Howard said. Then he turned to his daughter. "Take me to the lawyer you've been talking to."

Jessica blinked. "Papa?"

"I want to speak with him about Jacob's escape," Howard said, already moving. "And about the legal trouble still comin'. I intend to hire him both for Jacob's sake, and for Robert's."

"With your money?" Jessica was shocked.

"Yes, with mine," Howard said. "The Puckett family has been bled enough."

Martin watched them go, irritation burning hot in his chest.

They were slipping out of his hands.

Chapter 39

A few days later, Diana found Jessica waiting on the church steps for her, hands clasped so tightly her knuckles looked pale against the winter air.

"Well?" Diana asked before she could stop herself. "Did you go see the lawyer?"

Jessica nodded. "His office is above the dry goods store. He had shelves of books. You would have loved to see them." She smiled at her friend. "Papa said it smelled like dust and ink."

"Your father went?" Diana was shocked.

"He showed up at my dormitory with Deputy Martin. Martin thought I might have been in contact with Jacob, but of course I hadn't. I had no clue where he was, so Martin left to go to the depot to look for him. Papa went with me to see the lawyer. I don't know what exactly has caused his change of heart, but he thinks Jacob is innocent, Diana. He said your family has been through enough."

"Pastor Howard really said that?" Given the way that Pastor Howard had always acted toward her brother, and the way that he had preached against her father's alcoholism for all to hear, Diana couldn't believe it.

Jessica grinned as she nodded quickly. "It's an answered prayer. Wouldn't you say?"

"Of course," Diana agreed. "And what about the lawyer?"

"His name is W. R. Lovill. He was very professional. He stood when we walked in and shook our hands. Papa told him everything about the fire, Jacob's disappearance from the jail, and even your Pa's drinking. Did you know your Pa confessed to my father that he wanted to stop drinking and said he had started the fire?"

"Yes, Pastor Howard came to see us and told Ma and I."

"Well, did Papa say anything to y'all about Deputy Martin?" Jessica asked. "He's been trying to get my Pa to lay the blame on Robert for some time now."

Diana furrowed her brow. "No, but that doesn't surprise me. Martin and my Pa got in a fistfight a few weeks back. Martin didn't think my Pa was worthy of taking care of us. What did the lawyer say about Martin?"

"That Martin's name shows up at every turn of the story of what's happened to your family as of late, but that because he is a man of law, it complicates things."

"That's one way to put it." Diana sighed.

"When we told him that Deputy Martin went to the depot to look for Jacob, Mr. Lovill didn't like that either. Even so, he has agreed to take the cases, both Jacob's and Robert's."

Diana blinked. "Truly? Both of them?"

"Truly." Jessica's eyes shone. "He said he took Jacob's case because he doesn't like confessions given under pressure, and with the way that Deputy Martin has been acting, he likes even less the idea of a deputy shaping events to suit himself."

Diana hugged Jessica. "Oh, thank you, thank you, thank you for seeing the lawyer. We couldn't have done it without you."

"You know I'd do anything for you, Diana," Jessica said. "Your family is my family."

"So, what's next?" Diana asked.

"Mr. Lovill said that first we need to ensure Jacob's rights are preserved even in his absence. Secondly, we prepare to challenge Robert's new confession."

"What if Jacob is found?" Diana asked.

"Mr. Lovill said we'll insist on due process, not theatrics."

"Pray with me for a good outcome?" Diana asked. Jessica grabbed her hand, and the two young women bowed their heads.

***

Two weeks had passed, and the courthouse in Boone loomed larger than Diana expected, its stone walls damp with winter cold. She sat beside Jessica on the hard wooden bench, their coats folded tight around them, their knees nearly touching. The room smelled of wool and coal smoke and something else. Perhaps it was judgment.

Robert Puckett sat at the defense table, thinner than Diana remembered, sober-eyed and rigid. She wished her Ma were there, but Margaret had woken that morning weak and shaking. Her spells were worse in the cold. Diana had kissed her cheeks and promised to tell her everything.

At the front of the room stood Mr. Lovill, the lawyer. He did not look impressive at first glance. He did not have a booming voice or make dramatic gestures, but there was a steadiness to him that settled Diana's nerves. He shuffled his papers once, then rose.

The prosecution called their witnesses first. The testimony was thin and circumstantial, built more on Robert's reputation than fact. Martin sat behind the prosecution table, eyes fixed forward, his hands clenched together.

Then Mr. Lovill stood.

"Your Honor," he said calmly. "The defense calls Mr. John Miller."

A murmur rippled through the room as the manager of the Green Park Inn took the stand. Mr. Miller cleared his throat and spoke plainly about Robert's drinking, but also about Jacob trying to take his father home, and about Martin's presence that night.

"Did you see Mr. Puckett start a fire?" the lawyer asked.

"No, sir."

"Did you see him behave violently?"

"No, sir."

Mr. Lovill nodded. "Thank you."

The next witness made the room go very still.

A man Diana recognized only by reputation, one of the moonshiners from the hills, was sworn in.

"You've been granted immunity for your testimony today," Mr. Lovill said evenly. "Is that correct?"

"Yes, sir."

"Tell the court what Deputy Martin asked of you the week before the fire."

The man swallowed. "He asked for liquor that was stronger than usual."

Martin shifted in his seat.

"And did he say why?"

The man's voice shook. "He said Robert Puckett needed help forgettin'. He said he was gonna make sure folks believed Robert started the fire."

The courtroom erupted.

Martin sprang to his feet. "That's a lie!"

The judge slammed his gavel. "Order!"

But Martin was already moving.

Chapter 39

The crack of a gunshot ripped through the air.

Jessica screamed. Diana froze.

The bullet struck the wall behind the witness, splintering the wood. The man dove from the stand as Martin bolted for the door. Chairs were overturned. The police lunged after him, shouting.

Within moments, Martin was gone.

The judge stood, his face pale but firm. "This court has heard enough."

Hours later, or minutes, Diana couldn't tell, the verdict was read.

"Not guilty."

A sob broke from Diana's chest. Jessica clutched her hand.

The judge continued, "There is no evidence that Robert Puckett started the fire. He is free to go."

Robert sagged, covering his face with his hands.

As the room emptied, Diana thought of Ma at home, waiting by the window.

She could hardly wait to tell her the good news!

Chapter 40

They would look for him in the woods first.

Martin knew it as he ran. He knew the Boone and Blowing Rock police would ride straight for the moonshine stills, boots crunching through snow and leaves, thinking they had him cornered where the copper shone. That was where a guilty man would go.

So, Martin went a different way, to Margaret Puckett's house. Her cabin sat quiet against the gray afternoon, smoke curling from the chimney. He slowed only long enough to catch his breath before knocking, rapping just loud enough to sound urgent.

Margaret opened the door a crack. "Martin?" she said, surprised. "What are you doing here?"

He forced his voice steady. "I hate to bring bad news, Maggie, but I felt you ought to hear it from me."

She hesitated, then opened the door wider. "Come in, but call me Mrs. Puckett."

Martin ignored her comment about her surname. In a short time, he could convince her to become Mrs. Martin instead. The warmth hit him all at once. He took it in greedily, stepping inside as if he belonged there.

"The trial," he said quietly. "It ain't goin' well for Robert."

Margaret's hand went to her chest. "What do you mean?"

"The lawmen are saying the jury's leanin' hard against him. I didn't want you blindsided."

She shook her head. "Mr. Lovill told me he was hopeful."

Martin sighed, as if burdened by duty. "Lawyers always are, but I've seen these things turn."

He watched her closely and saw her fear bloom.

"Maggie," he said gently, stepping closer. "You don't have to wait for it to break you."

She looked up. "What are you sayin'?"

"I've made plans," Martin said. "I made investments so I'd have money put aside."

"In what?" she asked.

"Somethin' solid," he said quickly. "Enough to start fresh."

Her brow furrowed in confusion.

"Listen, I've got two tickets that are redeemable at the depot in Boone. The Tweetsie train will go to Johnson City. We'll cross the state line before sundown. No one in Tennessee will suspect a thing."

Margaret stared at him. "You're talkin' about runnin'."

"I'm talkin' about livin'," Martin insisted. "I'll get you a new doctor. One who knows what he's doing and will actually help you."

She stepped back. "No."

He blinked. "Maggie . . ."

"No," she repeated, firmer now. "I'm not leavin' my husband."

"Your husband's already lost," Martin said, the edge creeping in. "And you know it."

She lifted her chin. "Robert Puckett is a good man."

Martin laughed bitterly. "Good men don't let their families starve while they drown themselves."

Margaret's eyes flashed. "The difference between you and Robert is that Robert never put himself first. Not till the bottle, and even then, it was because he thought he couldn't do better . . . for me."

She took another step back, putting further distance between them.

"You have always put yourself first," she continued.

Martin's knees hit the floor before he knew he was moving.

"Maggie," he begged, clutching at her skirt. "I've loved you since we were children. I never understood why you chose him with me standin' right here."

She gently pulled free. "Love don't look like this."

He looked up at her, wild-eyed. "Come with me."

She shook her head. "Good riddance, Martin."

He stood, face hardening, the mask slipping at last. Without another word, he turned and walked out into the cold.

The road bent toward Glen Burney Falls.

Behind the roar of the water, tucked deep where the mist hid everything, Martin knew he had one last stash waiting.

He headed that way, the sound of the falls already rising in his ears, louder than his conscience.

Chapter 41

The verdict barely finished leaving the judge's mouth before Diana was on her feet.

She crossed the aisle in three quick steps and threw her arms around her father, pressing her face into his coat as if letting go might undo it all.

"Pa," she sobbed. "Pa, you're free."

Robert wrapped his arms around her, rough hands trembling against her back. For a moment he couldn't speak at all. When he did, his voice broke.

"Thank the Lord. Thank the Almighty Lord, my Savior."

The courtroom buzzed with voices. Men were talking all at once, but Diana heard only her father's breathing steady beside her.

They rode home slowly. The sheriff himself drove Robert and Diana back to Blowing Rock. He kept his gaze fixed ahead, as though ashamed to look at either of them.

"I was wrong," the sheriff said at last. "I trusted the wrong man. I'm sorry, Robert"

Robert nodded once. "I reckon we've all been wrong about somethin'."

***

Margaret was sitting up when they arrived, her eyes searching the doorway for the moment it would open.

"He won," Diana barged in breathlessly. "He won!"

Margaret gasped, then cried out softly as Robert crossed the room and took her into his arms. She clung to him.

"I knew the Lord wouldn't leave us," she said and planted a big kiss on his cheek.

When the tears eased, Margaret told the sheriff, "Martin was here."

Sheriff Critcher stiffened. "When?"

"Before the trial ended," Margaret replied. "He told me . . . well, I now know that he lied . . . that it was goin' against you." She looked at Robert as she said this. "He wanted me to run away with him."

Diana felt a chill. *Was this really what caused Robert's hatred of her father all this time? He was in love with her mother?*

"He talked about money," Margaret went on. "And said he had train tickets to Johnson City, Tennessee, but there was a secret place he needed to stop by first to pick up somethin' he'd hidden."

Robert frowned. "What place?"

"He didn't say," Margaret answered. "Just that it was hidden where no one would look. I bet it is money."

"Do you know where this place could be?" the sheriff asked Robert.

"No, I'm afraid not," Robert replied.

Outside, the wind picked up again, rattling the bare branches.

Martin was still out there.

Chapter 42

The sound of the falls came before the sign of them.

Martin slowed as he reached the tree line, his breath ragged and his boots slipping on wet leaves. Glen Burney Falls roared ahead, swollen with winter melt. The water hammered the rock with a violence that matched the pounding of his chest.

He was almost there when he heard voices.

Martin dropped low without thinking, pressing himself behind a rhododendron as two Blowing Rock policemen passed on the trail below.

"Sheriff says the road to Boone's closed now," one of them said. "No one's gettin' through till we find Martin."

Martin's stomach twisted

Boone was cut off. The train station was out of reach.

The men moved on, their footsteps fading, but the truth stayed sharp and cold: there was no clear way out now.

Martin rose slowly, and that was when he saw her.

Jessica Reece stood a little way down the path, bundled against the cold, her head bent in prayer. She looked small and unprotected against the trees.

An answer, sudden and terrible, settled over him.

She turned just as he reached her.

"Deputy Martin—" she began.

He clamped a hand over her mouth and dragged her backward into the brush. She fought him desperately, but he was stronger.

"Don't," he hissed in her ear. "Don't waste your breath. No one can hear you here."

He hauled her through the freezing water behind the falls, the roar swallowing every sound. The hidden cave opened up just as he remembered to crates, jars, and burlap sacks heavy with cash stacked where the mist kept them hidden.

Jessica stumbled, coughing and dripping with water, terror wide in her eyes.

"You know," Martin said almost conversationally as he grabbed a bag of money, "this trail you walked in on used to belong to the Indians. It ran clean through these mountains."

She shook violently.

"There was a story," he went on, tightening his grip, "about a Cherokee man who loved a maiden so much he'd follow her anywhere. You ever wonder if he walked this very path?"

Her eyes pleaded with him. She tried to scream again.

Martin slapped a hand over her mouth. "It don't matter. No one can hear you over the water falling."

He snapped his handcuffs around her wrists, tight enough to hurt, then wrapped cloth over her mouth. When he pulled her back out from behind the falls, he slung the bag of cash over his shoulder.

They walked fast. Martin pressed his gun to her head as the ground rose, the trees thinned, and the wind grew stronger. The Blowing Rock loomed ahead, the cliff's edge a dark promise against the gray sky.

"No one's takin' me alive," he said into her ear. "And if I go over that edge, you're goin' with me."

Jessica shook, tears streaming down her face

Martin stared ahead, jaw clenched.

The wind whipped harder as they reached the overlook, the legend pressing in on him of the Chickasaw girl, her lover's leap, and the mercy of the air that blew him back to her again.

But even as the thought crossed his mind, he knew the truth of it.

He loved Margaret. Not Jessica.

And love, real love, was the only thing that lifted people back up.

The wind howled, and Martin stood at the edge, holding on to the wrong woman, the woman Jacob Puckett loved.

Chapter 43

The knock came hard and fast, rattling the door frame.

Diana was the one who opened it.

Two Blowing Rock policemen stood on the porch, hats in hand, faces grim. Behind them was the sheriff.

"We found Deputy Martin," one of the officers said.

"Oh, good! Pa, Ma, they found Martin," she called back. Her parents came forward.

"But he's at the Blowing Rock," the sheriff added quickly. "He's got Jessica Reece."

Margaret cried out. Robert was already racing for his coat.

"Someone needs to alert Pastor Howard," Robert said.

"He's been told," the sheriff said. "He's on the way."

They did not waste another moment.

"I'm going with you Pa!" Diana called out. "Jessica's my best friend!"

"Alright," Robert said. "But stay behind me."

***

The wind at the Blowing Rock was merciless.

A few motorcars and some horses lined the narrow road, their presence useless against the sheer drop and roaring air. The crowd held back as the sheriff stepped forward, hand raised.

At the very edge of the cliff stood Martin.

Jessica was bound and gagged, one arm locked tight against his chest, her feet perilously close to the void.

"Don't y'all come any further!" Martin shouted at them "And if you shoot me, she goes with me over the edge."

Pastor Howard stepped out from the crowd, his coat snapping in the wind.

"Martin," he called, voice steady despite the fear written across his face. 'You don't have to end it this way. God will give you another chance. Come back."

Martin laughed, wild and hollow. "You talkin' about redemption, Pastor?" He shook his head. "I don't want redemption. I just want my freedom back!"

Howard took another step. "Please, let her go!"

Martin's eyes flicked to Robert Puckett as he emerged from the line of officers.

"I will," Martin said. "On two conditions."

The wind seemed to hold its breath.

"First, Robert Puckett takes her place."

Diana gasped. "Pa! No!"

"Second, you let me walk. I cross into Tennessee and never come back to North Carolina."

The sheriff hesitated.

Robert did not.

He stepped forward, his face set with a resolve Diana had not seen in years.

"Pa!" she cried.

Robert didn't look back. "Take care of your Ma if this goes badly," he said.

Martin tightened his grip on Jessica as Robert approached. With one hand raised and the other locked on Robert's sleeve, Martin eased them forward. Then, he shoved Jessica away.

Pastor Howard caught his daughter just in time, crushing her to his chest as she sobbed into his coat.

"I've got you," he whispered.

Martin turned his attention fully to Robert.

That was when the shot rang out.

Martin screamed as the bullet tore into his leg, his grip faltered, and his balance broke.

And in that instance, Robert Puckett went over the edge.

"Pa!" Diana's scream tore through the wind as the cliff swallowed him whole.

Chapter 44

Pain came first.

White-hot and blinding, it tore through Martin's leg and dropped him hard against the stone. The world tilted, spun, then slammed back into place as his shoulder struck the ground.

The gun flew from his hand. Boots were everywhere as hands wrenched his arms behind him.

Handcuffs bit into his wrists.

As they dragged him back from the ledge, Martin twisted his head to see that Robert Puckett disappeared.

A sound ripped out of Martin's chest. His laughter, wild and cracked, echoed against the rocks.

He laughed until his throat burned, until tears streamed from his eyes.

"He's gone," Martin gasped. "Finally gone!"

No one looked at him.

The sheriff had already sprinted to the edge with Diana right behind him. She dropped to her knees, clawing at the rock, peering down into the rocks below.

"Pa!" she screamed.

Martin craned his neck, still laughing at her incessant screaming.

Then the sheriff shouted, "I see him! He's holdin' on!"

Martin's laughter faltered.

Another officer rushed forward, dropped to his belly, grabbing the sheriff's belt as the sheriff reached over the edge. For a long, unbearable moment, the wind screamed louder than anything else.

Then Robert Puckett's body came up over the ledge, scraped and bleeding, but breathing. He collapsed onto the solid ground, coughing hard, clinging to the earth like it was a living thing.

Diana sobbed, falling against him. "Thank you, Lord," she cried.

Martin stared. The sound that came out of him this time was not laughter.

"On your feet," an officer snapped.

They hauled him to his feet with pain screaming through his legs and the cuffs cutting into his wrists.

Chapter 45

Jessica would not be dissuaded.

"I have to see him," she said, her voice steady in a way Diana knew cost her dearly. "I need to hear from his mouth why he took me."

So, Diana went with her. Deputy Martin sat on the bench inside the same jail cell that had once held both Jacob and Robert Puckett, bundled in a blanket, his leg splinted, and his face drawn and hollow.

When he saw them, his mouth twitched, almost like a snarl.

Jessica stepped up to the bars. "Why did you take me?" she asked.

Martin laughed softly. "Because I knew it'd make your daddy mad."

Jessica flinched, but held her ground.

"And because no one in Blowing Rock wants to see the pastor's daughter die. Not like they'd shrug if it was someone else."

Jessica swallowed. "You talked about the Indians at the falls before you took me to the Blowing Rock. Tell me why."

Martin leaned against the wall. "There was a story," he said. "A Cherokee man loved a Chickasaw maiden. When he leapt from the Blowing Rock, the wind carried him back. Her love saved him."

Jessica shook her head slowly. "That doesn't make any sense. We don't love each other."

The words hung there.

Something clicked in Diana's mind. Martin at their house. His pleading with her mother to go with him to Tennessee.

"No," Diana said. "It wasn't her you loved."

Martin's eyes snapped to her.

"You loved my Ma," Diana went on. "But she turned you away."

His hands shot out, gripping the bars so hard his knuckles went white. "You don't know nothin'."

"If you loved my ma, then why did you take my brother, her son? You must have done it."

"For the last time, I don't know where that boy is!" Martin shouted, rattling the bars. "He ruined everything. He wasn't supposed to disappear."

Sheriff Critcher stood from his desk. "That's enough."

He ushered the girls outside, closing the door gently behind them.

Outside, he said, "I hate to say this, but I believe Jacob may be dead."

Jessica gasped. Diana's knees nearly gave way.

"I think Martin threw him from the Blowing Rock weeks ago," the sheriff continued, "And if that's so, there may not be much left to find. Animals would've . . ."

"No," Jessica sobbed. "It can't be true."

Diana shook her head, tears blinding her. "Please," she begged. "You have to look."

The sheriff's voice softened. "The cliffs are iced over. It ain't safe. We'll have to wait till spring."

Spring.

How could such a lively word suddenly sound so cruel?

Chapter 46

The snow finally let up enough for folks to come out. Their shoes crunched along the white-packed paths toward church. Smoke curled from chimneys, and the church bells rang clear and hopeful, as if they, too, had been holding their breath these past weeks.

Inside, the sanctuary was full.

Pastor Howard stood at the pulpit longer than usual before he spoke. His Bible lay open, but his hands rested flat on the wood, steadying himself.

"Church," he said quietly. "Today I'm preaching on mercy."

He spoke of bearing one another's burdens, of how easy it is to watch a family fall apart from a distance and call judgment righteousness. He spoke of helping the broken instead of gossiping about them, and of lifting people up when they are down rather than measuring how far they've fallen.

Then he swallowed.

"I need to confess something to you," he said. "I watched the Puckett family struggle. I saw pride, anger, and sin. I also saw pain, and instead of stepping in with love and compassion, I stood back and judged. I told myself Robert Puckett brought it on himself." His voice broke. "I was wrong."

"If we wait until someone deserves help," Pastor Howard continued, "we will never help anyone at all. Christ didn't wait. And neither should we."

The words settled heavy and honest in the room.

When the altar call came, Diana rose and knelt at the front.

She prayed for Jacob. Not for closure due to his possible death, but for answers, and for his life.

She still believed, deep in her heart, that her brother was alive somewhere.

The congregation began to sing, the hymn "Amazing Grace," rising. Diana stayed where she was, praying through every verse. She felt her father kneel beside her, then Jessica on her other side. Together, they bowed their heads and made up a small circle of faith.

Then Diana looked up.

A Blowing Rock police officer had entered quietly and walked down the aisle. He leaned close and whispered something into Pastor Howard's ear.

Pastor Howard's face changed for the better.

He threw his hands into the air and hollered, "Hallelujah!"

The singing stopped mid-verse. A ripple of startled murmurs ran through the church.

Pastor Howard laughed, his joy spilling over. "Deputy Martin can hurt us no more," he called out. "He's been transferred to Craggy Prison in Asheville!"

The church erupted in voices shouting praise and hands clapping. Diana felt her father's arm around her shoulders.

Pastor Howard waited for the noise to settle. Then, smiling wide, he stepped away from the pulpit.

He reached down and opened a trap door.

A gasp swept through the sanctuary as a head appeared, then shoulders, then a familiar, unmistakable grin.

"Jacob!" someone cried.

Jacob Puckett climbed into the light, smiling bright as that Sunday morning.

His family surged forward. Margaret sobbed his name. Jessica threw her arms around him. Diana clutched him so tight she thought her heart might burst.

"Where were you, Jacob?" Diana asked through tears.

He laughed softly. "Pa asked Pastor Howard to help me," he said. "He let me outta jail and kept me hidden right here in God's sanctuary. I worshiped with y'all every Sunday for weeks. Y'all just didn't know it."

Diana pressed her hands to her face, overwhelmed, then threw her hands in the air.

"Hallelujah! Praise the Lord!" she called out just as Pastor Howard had done.

And the whole church said, "Amen!"

Epilogue

Six months later, summer lay warm and green over the Blue Ridge Mountains, as if winter had never dared to claim them.

The air smelled of honeysuckle and fresh-cut hay, and laughter drifted across the churchyard where white ribbons fluttered from the fence posts. Jessica stood beneath the maple tree, sunlight dancing in her hair, Jacob's hand steady in hers. They looked older somehow. They looked tested, but whole.

Diana watched them and smiled.

Tomorrow, they would be married.

Today, Diana was packing.

Her satchel leaned against the porch rail, already filled with books and one good dress Margaret had mended twice over. Boone waited for her now, and the Training School she had once only dared to imagine. It still felt unreal to her, like a door God had quietly opened while she wasn't looking.

Pa came up beside Diana, steady again in his uniform. The sheriff's badge caught the light when he moved. Seeing him wear it once more still made Diana's chest ache in the best way.

"Hard to believe, ain't it?" he said, watching Jacob laugh as someone clapped him on the shoulder.

"No," she answered truthfully. "It feels like exactly where we're meant to be."

Margaret sat nearby, her color stronger than it had been in years. The doctor said it was the care, real care, that made the difference. Industrialist Moses Cone himself had stepped forward after the trial. His name was spoken with reverence around Blowing Rock given the summer home he had built there. He had seen the injustice against the Puckett family and opened his pockets without hesitation. Because of him, their Ma would live.

Because of grace, they all would.

Pastor Howard moved more slowly now. He smiled often and listened more than he spoke. He had announced his retirement not long ago, and his voice was peaceful as he said it. When Jessica and Jacob returned from their honeymoon, Jacob would take up the pulpit.

He had never wanted a badge.

He had always wanted a calling.

As the sun dipped low, painting the mountains gold, Diana thought of all that had been lost and all that had been restored. She thought of judgment turned into mercy and of Pastor Howard opening that trap door when hope seemed nearly gone.

Tomorrow, Jessica would be a wife.

Tomorrow, Diana would be a student.

And tonight, under the wide North Carolina sky, Diana whispered a prayer of thanks for the God who met them, not when they were worthy, but when they were willing.

The mountains stood quiet and faithful around them.

Now, so did their hearts.

Scriptures Referenced

In Order of Appearance

"The proud have hid a snare for me, and cords; they have spread a net by the wayside; they have set gins for me. Selah."

—Psalm 140:5

"Wine is a mocker, strong drink is raging; and whosoever is deceived thereby is not wise."

—Proverbs 20:1

"Behold, thou desirest truth in the inward parts: and in the hidden parts thou shalt make me know wisdom."

—Psalm 51:6

"The Lord will perfect that which concerneth me: thy mercy, O LORD, endureth for ever: forsake not the works of thine own hands."

—Psalm 138:8

Biblical Note

The Holler was inspired by the life of the Biblical King David. I have always found David's story particularly fascinating. He was chosen by God to rule as king, chosen while still a shepherd boy, and called "a man after God's own heart" in 1 Samuel 13:14. Yet, Scripture does not soften his failures. David was courageous and faithful, but also deeply flawed. He was capable of terrible sin as well as genuine repentance. That tension between divine calling and human weakness is what drew me to use his story as an inspiration for *The Holler*.

In particular, David's lust for Bathsheba and his decision to orchestrate the death of her husband Uriah, a loyal soldier and perhaps even David's colleague inspired the character of Deputy Martin. Like David, Martin allows jealousy, desire, and pride to curdle into betrayal, using his position of authority to conceal wrongdoing.

Likewise, David's season of hiding in the cave from King Saul inspired Jacob's disappearance and his refuge beneath the church. Just as David cried out to God from the darkness, praying for deliverance while hunted by someone he once trusted, Jacob's disappearance reveals fear, and his surprise appearance later on reveals the truth of God's protection.

Through these parallels, it is my hope that *The Holler* seeks to echo the Biblical truth that God works even through broken people and grievous sin. He does not excuse evil, but He does bring what is hidden into the light. David's life reminds us that consequences are real, and yet, grace remains possible.

Historical Note

This story is especially meaningful to me because it is set in my own county. These mountains, towns, and hollers are not merely a setting. They're my home. While *The Holler* is a work of fiction, it is deeply rooted in the real people, places, and events that shaped Watauga County, North Carolina, and the surrounding High Country.

Several historical details appear throughout this novella, sometimes accurately, and sometimes with my intentional creative license.

The fire that devastated Blowing Rock's business district in 1923 truly did happen. Historically, however, it was never caused by a person. It was an accidental electrical fire that caused all the businesses on one side of Main Street to burn down. The destruction ultimately led Blowing Rock to establish its first fire department.

Mount Bethel remains the oldest church in Blowing Rock. It was built in 1886 by Jacob Kluttz as a German Reformed church. Its denomination has changed several times over the years, and it is no longer being used for services. The church remains in the care of the Kluttz family who has been working on restoring it. It is a small white church with a few steps at the front.

Appalachian Training School is known today as Appalachian State University. It began in 1899 as

Watauga Academy, a school for teachers. In 1903, its name changed to Appalachian Training School, and it began offering two-year degrees. In 1925, the name would change again to Appalachian Normal School, though the teaching curriculum and two-year degree program remained the same. A few years later, in 1929, the name changed to Appalachian State Teachers College. Then, finally, in 1967, it became a four-year college, Appalachian State University. The school's evolution mirrors the growth of the region itself that continues to this day. Unfortunately, though, the region's growth has led to the destruction of the Green Park Inn. Though it was on the National Register of Historic Places, it was torn down in 2025. Condominiums and a new hotel will be built in its place.

The Green Park Inn never actually sold illegal moonshine, at least not that I could prove. During the Prohibition Era, however, many inns that once had bars continued to operate their restaurants, often skirting the spirit, if not the letter of the law. I took creative license here to reflect the atmosphere of the time rather than a specific documented act.

Ironically, while *The Holler* was in developmental editing, another Blowing Rock business, a restaurant called Bistro Roca caught fire and burned. Bistro Roca was home to Antlers Bar, the oldest continuously operating bar in the state of North Carolina. Antlers Bar opened nearly a decade after the Blowing Rock business district fire and began serving liquor and beer in 1932. The Prohibition Era did not end until the ratification of the 21st amendment in 1933, a year later. The 21st amendment led to the repeal of the 18th amendment that began prohibition on the production, importation, transportation, and sale of alcoholic beverages across the United States beginning in 1920. Having opened just before Prohibition's end, Antlers Bar operated as a speakeasy. Even though the national ban on liquor was lifted in 1933, North Carolina kept the ban in place across the state until 1935. I suspect, though I have been unable to prove, that local law enforcement was aware of the business's illegal sale of liquor and let it slide.

In 1908, North Carolina actually became the first southern state to enact statewide prohibition of alcoholic beverages, and though the state ban was lifted in 1935, many Watauga County residents would remain adamant that the drink should be banned once again. An article from January 21, 1943, in the *Watauga Democrat* reported that, "the Dry Forces of Watauga county met at the First Baptist church on Monday, January 18, and resolutions were presented to back up the county and town officers of the law in their work, and at the same time to put on a campaign of education in the churches on the evils of drink." Their main concern was that "drunken driving cases were eleven times more than in dry years." However, they did not specifically target liquor. The article explains that petitions were "being put out over the county by the preachers and the churches and other workers for the citizens to sign, to put wine and beer out of the county."[1]

Moonshining, however, remained very real in North Carolinian and Appalachian history. Long before Prohibition, distilling spirits was a legitimate way for farmers to earn an income, especially in rugged mountain terrain where the success of crops varied due to frosts and frozen ground. This tradition later became famous through NASCAR legend Junior Johnson in neighboring Wilkes County, where fast cars were used to outrun revenue agents, eventually giving rise to organized stock car racing. Johnson was convicted of moonshining in 1956, but President Ronald Reagan later pardoned him in 1986.

The No. 12 train that carried students into Boone from Johnson City, Tennessee, was called Tweetsie, named this by locals because its high-pitched whistle makes a "tweet, tweet" sound. In 1919, the East Tennessee & Western North Carolina line was expanded into Boone, North Carolina. The train was in operation until a flood caused the destruction of the railway in 1940. After that, Tweetsie operated on the Shenandoah Central Railroad for a while before the singing cowboy, Gene Autry, purchased her with the intention of shipping the train to California for use in movies. In 1956, Blowing Rock resident, Grover Robbins, bought Tweetsie from Autry for one dollar and brought her back home. Today, the train lives on as Tweetsie Railroad, North Carolina's first theme park, which opened in 1957. The detail of including the train depot is especially personal to me, as I worked at Tweetsie Railroad for three years in the antique photo parlor as an Appalachian State University college student.

In reality, the sheriff's office and jail were located in Boone, not Blowing Rock. Boone is the county seat. I chose to place the sheriff's office in Blowing Rock for narrative reasons, primarily to give Deputy Martin more time in Blowing Rock and to simplify the complex communication barriers that existed historically, particularly when deputies had jurisdiction over the entire county.

Those communication barriers were not insignificant. One of the most tragic consequences of limited communication was the murder of Blowing Rock Police Chief William Dean Greene, Sr., in 1962, nearly four decades after the infamous Blowing Rock fire took place. Chief Greene was killed while investigating a robbery. Though he radioed for backup, the sheriff's office, despite being geographically closer, did not receive his call for help. Instead, police in a neighboring county received the call, but help did not arrive in time. His death prompted critical improvements in the communication system, and today, a bronze plaque in the Blowing Rock Town Hall commemorates his sacrifice and service.

The legend of the Blowing Rock itself is still fondly remembered by locals. While the story is unlikely to be historically accurate in its details, it does reflect on an important truth: Watauga County was originally Cherokee land. Today, the Blowing Rock attraction is operated by the current Blowing Rock mayor, Charlie Sellers, who is a cousin to the man who owns Tweetsie Railroad, Chris Robbins, grandson to Grover Robbins. Charlie Sellers is Grover Robbins' great-grandson. The Blowing Rock is also recognized as North Carolina's oldest tourist attraction.

Finally, while the setting and many historical references are real, all main characters in this novel are entirely fictional. Some supporting figures, including the sheriff, the lawyer, and Moses Cone, are real historical individuals. Moses Cone's home, now controlled by the National Park Service, still stands and can be visited today.

As with all historical fiction, *The Holler* blends fact and imagination. My hope is that the story honors the spirit of Watauga County's struggles and its legacies.

1. J.C. Canipe, "Dry Forces Meet; Says Crime Rises During Wet Era," *Watauga Democrat*, January 21, 1943, Digital NC, https://newspapers.digitalnc.org/lccn/sn82007642/1943-01-21/ed-1/seq-1/.

Acknowledgements

This book would not exist without the help, generosity, and encouragement of many people and organizations.

My sincere gratitude goes to Appalachian State University, the Appalachian Regional Library, the Digital Watauga Project, The Blowing Rock, Tweetsie Railroad, the Watauga Democrat, and the High Country Press, for their resources which proved invaluable to my research for the creation of this story. In particular, I'd like to thank the Richard Trexler Collection, the Bobby Brendell Postcard Collection, and the Blowing Rock Historical Society for their photographic contributions to Digital Watauga.

Photographs of materials in these collections appear in the special edition paperback of The Holler.

To my family, endorsers, ARC readers, and my wonderful #bookstagram friends, thank you for cheering me on, sharing posts, and reminding me why my stories matter. Your support means more than I could ever put into words.

A special thank you goes to Madisyn Carlin of Mountain Peak Edits & Design for creating a beautiful cover and for offering thoughtful developmental editing. Your talents are a gift!

Thank you, Abigail Timm of Servant's Song Publishing Services & Christian Fiction, for careful copyediting and formatting, and for helping bring clarity and polish to every page!

Most of all, thank you, God, who gave me the calling and the idea to write another book.

My prayer is that somewhere in reading these pages, someone will be reminded that they are more than their mistakes and give Him a chance.

Request for Reviews

Thank you so much for taking the time to read *The Holler*. Since I live in Watauga County, *The Holler* is extra special to me. I'm glad that through writing this novella, I have been able to share a little of my local history with you. If you enjoyed reading *The Holler*, I would be grateful if you would post a review. Your review not only helps make me a better writer, but also helps readers discover this story.

Newsletter

For sneak peeks, exclusive giveaways, early-bird book reviews, and other fun events and updates, be sure to follow me on Instagram @alicemondayauthor and subscribe to my newsletter! You can find it on my website, https://authoralicemonday.com.

Available Now

Winner of the 2025 Christlit Book Award

Set during the American Civil War, Elizabeth Parks renounces her faith in God in the wake of her husband's sudden death by yellow fever. Feeling lonely and trapped, she throws herself into the nursing of wounded soldiers following the First Battle of Bull Run on July 21, 1861, and hopes she will find some comfort in helping others. When a gravely injured drummer boy soldier named Samuel Gordon arrives at

Charlottesville General Hospital, Elizabeth finds purpose in nursing the child back to health so that he can make it home for Christmas.

With Samuel's Christmas wish driving her forward, Elizabeth leaves her home in Virginia to accompany Samuel back to his father's home in Maryland where he hopes to play his drum for his father, Thomas. Along the way, war and loss continues to threaten them at every turn, but Elizabeth also catches a glimmer of hope against such suffering as Samuel relays Bible stories, including the story of Jesus's birth, to Elizabeth. When they finally reach Samuel's father, Thomas, Elizabeth's heart begins to heal. As she helps care for Samuel and spends time with Thomas, Elizabeth questions whether she should remain in mourning or open her heart to new love and embrace the peace that only comes through trusting in His plan.

Inspired by the song, "The Little Drummer Boy," *So, To Honor Him* released on October 27, 2025. It is part of *The Carols of Christmas*, a multi-author series, though it can be read as a standalone novella.

About the Author

Jewel Parker is a history instructor who chose Alice Monday as a pen name to honor her great-grandmother and to separate her fiction from her academic publications. Over time, Jewel realized that her pen name was important for another reason—the glory of writing and publishing was not for herself, but for God.

Jewel holds a Ph.D. in History from the University of North Carolina at Greensboro, and a GO Certificate in Biblical Studies and Theology from Southeastern Baptist Theological Seminary. She incorporates both history and theology in her fictional works.

www.ingramcontent.com/pod-product-compliance
Lightning Source LLC
La Vergne TN
LVHW090517110826
845146LV00003B/895

* 9 7 9 8 9 9 2 5 4 5 8 3 8 *